The Perfect Christmas

Christmas 2009

Dear Friends,

I've always enjoyed writing romantic comedies, especially those with a Christmas theme. And what could be funnier than a "perfect" Christmas? I'm sure you know why I smile every time I think about it. Because a perfect Christmas (at least in *my* experience) simply doesn't exist. My heroine, like me, gazes at those lovely family-photo Christmas cards with a sense of awe—everything looks so...well, perfect. This is what Cassie wants, and she's determined to make it happen. And so the fun begins....

I've always believed there's a special connection between the writer and the reader, a connection revealed through the characters and the story. If I cry, I know you will, too. If I laugh, so will you. Well, I want to tell you that I laughed my way through this book. Every story should be this much fun to write!

In case you're interested in what Christmas in the Macomber household is like, let me give you an idea. I put up a Christmas tree for every family—five in total—so the grandkids know which tree belongs to them. I've lost count of the number of Nativity sets I have all over the house. Some are large and ornate, others small and fragile. A few have missing pieces, but we've always managed to find the baby Jesus. Then there's the entertaining. I host several Christmas teas, potlucks and a progressive dinner, plus I arrange cooking-with-Grandma sessions for the grandkids. In other words, it's pretty chaotic around our house in December. Wayne and the dog have been known to hide in the basement for a good part of the month.

Yet, despite the chaos (and having to haul husband and dog back upstairs), that's about as perfect as Christmas gets for me. I surround myself with family and friends. You can be sure there'll be plenty of home-baked goodies and a glass of eggnog for all.

By the way, the Southcenter Mall and the Tacoma Mall are real—and both are shopping centers I visit often—but my versions of them in this story reflect my own imagination as much as the actual places.

If you're looking for a few hours of escape from the Christmas craziness this year, then sit down by the tree or the fireplace and lose yourself in *The Perfect Christmas.* (Let me know if Cassie's Christmas—or mine—is anything like yours. You can reach me at www.debbiemacomber.com or P.O. Box 1458, Port Orchard, WA 98366.)

Merry Christmas!

Debbie Macomber

DEBBIE MACOMBER

The Perfect Christmas

ISBN-13: 978-0-7783-2682-3

THE PERFECT CHRISTMAS

www.MIRABooks.com

Printed in U.S.A.

First Printing: October 2009
10 9 8 7 6 5 4 3 2 1

To

Gary and Marsha Roche

And

Bob Mullen

Who have shared their love of

Civil War history

With Wayne and me

Chapter 1

"Who mails out Christmas cards before Thanksgiving?" Cassie Beaumont lamented to her best friend.

Angie Barber looked up from her microscope and seemed to take an extra moment to consider what Cassie had just said. "You got a Christmas card? Already?"

Cassie wheeled her chair back to her station. "Can you believe it?"

"Who from?"

"An old college friend. You wouldn't know her." Cassie shrugged. "Jill married Tom two weeks after we graduated."

"They have children?"

Cassie caught the wisp of longing in Angie's voice and answered with a nod. "Two, a boy and a girl, and of course they're adorable."

"Of course," Angie echoed.

The Christmas card photo showed the four of them in matching outfits of green and red. The mother and daughter wore full-length green dresses with red-and-green plaid skirts. Father and son had on three-piece suits with vests in the same fabric as the dress skirts. It was too adorable for words.

"There was a letter, as well."

"Everything in their lives is perfect, right?" Angie asked.

"Perfect in every way," Cassie grumbled. The unfairness of it all was too much. Jill, who worked as a financial planner, held down a forty-hour-a-week job, kept a meticulous house and *still* managed to be a terrific wife and mother. Despite all the demands on her time, she'd mailed out her Christmas cards a full month in advance.

"Is there a reason the perfect Jill sent her Christmas cards so soon?" Angie asked.

"Jill and Tom just moved into a new home and wanted to update family and friends with their address change. Oh, and there was a photo of the house and it was—"

"Perfect," Angie finished for her.

"Perfect doesn't begin to describe it."

Angie watched her closely. "Do I detect a slight note of envy?" she asked.

"Slight envy? Me?" Cassie asked, exaggerating the words. "Heavens, no. What you're hearing is a full-blown case of jealousy. The green-eyed monster is alive and well." Cassie rolled her chair to the end of a counter filled with an assortment of microscopes, test tubes, slides and other equipment, then stood, hands propped on her hips. "Do you realize how long it's been since I've been on a real date?"

"You went out with Greg last week," Angie reminded her.

"Greg isn't a man," Cassie blurted out. "I mean, he is, but not in the sense of someone I'm interested in," she said. "Greg's...completely unsuitable as marriage material." She didn't need to explain that, at thirty-four, the ticking of her biological clock got louder by the year.

Angie sighed. "I agree."

He was eligible in practically every way but he happened to be divorced and in love with his ex-wife. Unfortunately, he hadn't figured that out yet. The entire date, if it could even be called a date, was spent rehashing the tragedy of his divorce. He went on and on about how much he missed his three kids—and his ex-wife, if the number of times he mentioned her name was any indication. The night had been sheer drudgery for Cassie. It was her first and last date with Greg.

"The problem is, we don't meet many guys here at work," Angie said. Cassie was well aware of that. Since they were holed up in a lab eight to ten hours a day, working as biochemists for a plastics company, the opportunities to socialize outside the job were limited.

"What really hit home," Cassie said, "after receiving that Christmas card, is how badly I want a family of my own."

"I know." The longing was back in Angie's voice, too.

"I don't understand why it's so hard to meet men. I'm reasonably attractive, right?"

Angie nodded enthusiastically. "Yes."

"Thirty-four isn't so old, is it?"

"Not really."

Cassie shook her head and wondered why she was still single. She *wanted* to be married, and she liked to think she had the full package—five-five, dark hair, dark eyes. She was attractive, as Angie had confirmed, and she was smart, with a successful career, an engaging personality (if she did say so herself) and plenty of friends. "I blame my mother for this."

"Your mother?"

"I blame my father, too, even if he didn't stick around all that long."

"Or maybe *because* he didn't stick around."

"Yeah, I guess. After the divorce, my mother was so down on marriage, the whole idea terrified me."

"But it doesn't anymore, does it?"

"No. I want a husband and I'd really like children." She grinned. "The ironic thing is, my mother's remarried."

"Marriage seems to terrify your brother, too. Shawn should be married by now, don't you think? He's older than you are."

"I'm not so sure about Shawn." Cassie sometimes wondered if Angie might be interested in her brother. There was actually nothing to indicate that, but every once in a while Cassie had this *feeling*.... "He travels so much that maintaining a long-term relationship would be difficult for him."

"True," Angie said.

Shawn was a well-known artist who painted murals all over the country. Brother and sister were close and kept in touch, calling each other two and three times a week. Currently Shawn was in Boca Raton, Florida, painting the side of a building that stood next to the freeway. He'd sent her photos of the mural from his cell phone—an ocean scene, which Cassie knew was his favorite. Whales rising up out of the crashing waves. Dolphins and sea turtles and all kinds of fish frolicked in the sparkling blue water. His murals made headlines wherever he went and huge crowds showed up to watch him paint.

"Shawn's a different case," Cassie said. In her opinion, that summed up the situation pretty accurately.

"But if you were married, I bet he'd show some interest in finding a wife," Angie commented.

Cassie had never thought of their family dynamic in those terms. Perhaps, in some obscure way, Shawn *was* waiting for her to make the leap first. Angie might be right. It wasn't that Shawn followed her lead—far from it. They'd both been traumatized by the divorce and by their mother's reaction. Their father, who wanted his kids to call him Pete, had been in and out of their lives. Mostly out and yet…yet he'd had a powerful influence on his children, whom he rarely recognized as such.

"Shawn won't feel marriage is safe until he sees *you* happily married," Angie went on to say.

Cassie scowled at her friend. "What makes you so smart?"

"Just an observation," Angie said. "I may not be correct, but it seems to me that you and Shawn are afraid of love."

"Me afraid of love? Hardly." Not if the longing in her heart was anything to go by. Like her friend Jill, she wanted it all.

"Whenever you meet a man—no matter how perfect he is—you find fault with him," Angie said.

Now, *that* was categorically untrue. "Not so," Cassie argued.

"Oh, it's all wine and roses in the beginning, but then it's over before you even have a chance to really know the guy."

"How can you say that?"

"Well, mostly," Angie told her softly, "I can say it because I've seen you do it again and again."

"You're not talking about me and Jess, are you? The man had no class. He scratched his private parts in public!"

"Not Jess."

"Who do you mean, then?"

"Rod."

Cassie cocked her head. "Rod? Rod who?"

"I don't remember his last name. You went out with him a year ago."

"Not Rod Showers? Good grief, he was so cheap I had to pay for my half of the meal and tip the valet because he refused to do it."

"What about Charles..."

Cassie got the point quickly enough. "Okay, okay, so I have standards."

"High standards."

"Okay, fine. High standards." Cassie had made the effort, though. "I've *tried* to meet men."

"We both have."

"I had hopes for that online dating service." The advertisements had looked so promising. Cassie and Angie had signed up together and then waited expectantly to meet their perfect matches.

It didn't happen.

"I had real hopes for that, too," Angie returned sadly. "I thought for sure we'd meet really wonderful husbands."

Cassie sighed. That had been an expensive venture. Her expectations had been great and her disappointment greater. Angie's too. In fact, Angie was the one who'd suggested trying the Internet.

"The church singles group was a good idea," she said now.

"A great idea," Cassie concurred, "if there'd been any men involved." They'd gone there to discover the group consisted of thirty women and two men—both close to retirement age.

Angie nodded. "The pickings were few and far between."

"We've read all the right books," Cassie said. "*Dating for Dummies. How to Find a Man in Five Easy Lessons.* My personal favorite was *Lasso Yourself a Husband and Other Ways to Make a Man Notice You.*"

"The only thing we managed to lasso was a hundred-dollar credit-card bill for all those books."

"Divided two ways," Cassie reminded her.

"They did make for interesting reading."

"They would've been a lot more interesting if we'd been able to make any of them work," Cassie said in acerbic tones.

"Yeah…"

"We've tried everything."

"I'm not giving up," Angie insisted. "And I won't let you give up, either."

Cassie sighed.

She was close to it. The Christmas card from Jill and Tom was the final straw. For too long she'd been convinced that one day soon, she'd be mailing glossy Christmas cards to all *her* friends and relatives. She, too, would have a photograph that showed the perfect husband, the perfect children, a boy and a girl, all looking forward to the perfect Christmas. But year after year it was the same. No husband. No children. And each Christmas with her embittered mother more depressing than the one before.

The time had come to step forward and find a man, she decided with new resolve. Maybe she did need to lower her standards. She couldn't allow another Christmas to pass without—

"There's something, or rather someone, you *haven't* tried," Angie said, cutting into Cassie's thoughts.

Cassie perked up. "Oh?"

Angie grew strangely quiet.

Cassie frowned. "Don't hold out on me now, Angie."

"He's expensive."

"How expensive? No, wait, don't tell me." She paused. "Who is this *he?*"

"A matchmaker."

"A matchmaker," Cassie repeated slowly. "I didn't know there was such a thing in this day and age."

"There is." Angie avoided eye contact. "In fact, more and more people are turning to professional matchmakers. It works, too—most of the time."

"Now tell me how expensive he is."

"Thirty thousand dollars."

"What?"

"You heard me—and apparently he's worth it."

"And you know about him because..." Cassie let the question hang between them.

"Because I went to him."

Cassie slapped her hands against her sides. "Clearly you wasted your money."

"It didn't cost me a dime."

"And why is that?"

Angie's gaze darted in every direction except Cassie's. "He wouldn't accept me as a client."

"He rejected you?" The man was nuts! Angie was lovely and smart and a thousand other adjectives that flew through her mind. "What's wrong with this guy, anyway?"

"He was right.... I'm not a good candidate and I would've been wasting my money."

"Why didn't you tell me about him before?"

"I...I didn't want anyone to know I'd been turned down."

"If he rejected you, then he'll probably reject me, too."

"No...he said he couldn't accept me because I have feelings for someone else."

"Do you?"

"I did—a long time ago," she said without elaborating further. "But don't let my experience dissuade you. Check him out. Like you said earlier, you've tried everything else. At least make an appointment and see what he has to say."

Cassie was tempted to ask more about this man Angie had feelings for, but her friend had clearly signalled an unwillingness to talk about it. As far as the matchmaker went, she wasn't convinced. "He actually does this for a living?"

"Yes. He has an office and an assistant. I asked him for his credentials and he has an advanced degree in psychology and—" Angie stared directly at her "—he guarantees his work."

"Guarantees?"

"Yes. If he doesn't find you a husband, you get a full refund. So make an appointment and see for yourself. Remember—nothing ventured, nothing gained."

"I'll consider it," Cassie said. She hated to admit that the idea intrigued her. Then again, it *was* rather archaic. Besides, if this man had rejected Angie, he couldn't be any good. Still it was an opportunity, and nothing else had presented itself.

When she got to her condo building that evening, Cassie stopped at her mailbox in the lobby and immediately noticed that her newspaper was missing. No surprise there. It vanished every Tuesday when the shopping ads came out. Her neighbor Mrs. Mullinex, took it, although Cassie hadn't been able to prove that yet. On Wednesday mornings, her paper mysteriously reappeared with the coupons clipped out. Twice now, Cassie had met her neighbor in the lobby. The grandmotherly woman didn't resemble a thief and would've been above suspicion if not for the handful of coupons she clutched in her gloved fingers.

Grumbling under her breath, Cassie headed for her apartment. She tossed the mail on the kitchen counter without looking. The picture of Jill, Tom and their two children smiled at her from the refrigerator door.

The perfect family having the perfect Christmas.

Jill's smile seemed to be telling Cassie "All this could be yours, too."

"A matchmaker?" Cassie said aloud. "Am I really resorting to this?"

Angie had given Cassie his business card and then for good measure a hug and parting words of advice. "Just do it. I don't think you'll be sorry."

Cassie hesitated and glanced over at the perfect family posed in front of the world's most beautiful Christmas tree. Oh, for heaven's sake, what would it hurt?

After rummaging around the bottom of her purse, she found the engraved card that read: Dr. Simon Dodson, Professional Matchmaker.

Heart pounding, Cassie reached for the phone.

Chapter 2

Simon says: A good matchmaker *always* knows his clients—especially after a background check!

Cassie had to wait a week before she could get an appointment with Simon Dodson. He made sure she understood that he was doing her a favor by squeezing her in at the end of the day. All right, to be fair, his personal assistant, Ms. Snelling, a rather unpleasant woman, made it sound as if an appointment was a terrible inconvenience. Frankly Cassie didn't hold out much hope for this, and who could blame her? The matchmaking psychologist had declined to accept Angie, who was probably the most decent, kindest person Cassie had ever known.

The day of the appointment, Cassie went home to change clothes. She dressed carefully, choosing a suit that made her look confident but not formal, and she refreshed her makeup. When she walked into his office, it was with her head held high. She'd done her homework and was keeping an open mind. She'd checked two references the Snelling woman had passed on and felt she knew what to expect. Both couples had raved about Simon. The wives had warned her that Dr. Dodson wasn't the "warm and fuzzy" type. One of them had suggested that Cassie should be patient and not take offense. Hmm...that was unusual advice.

"Dr. Dodson will see you shortly," his assistant informed her primly after Cassie announced herself. The office had modern art decorating the walls, large green plants in the corners and soft leather furniture in a deep shade of brown.

"You filled out the paperwork I e-mailed you and brought it in?"

"Yes, I have it here." Cassie thought applying for a job at the CIA would've been easier. Simon was interested in every aspect of her background, from the name of her first-grade teacher to her current shoe size. Okay, maybe that was an exaggeration—a slight one—but she didn't see how most of the questions were relevant. Really, why did Simon need a list of any allergies she might have?

She handed the lengthy application form to the assistant, who scanned it, then took it into the inner office. Ms. Snelling reappeared a couple of minutes later and gave her a thorough once-over. Then, to Cassie's surprise, the woman offered her a reassuring smile.

Cassie studied the assistant. She guessed Ms. Snelling was in her late fifties; she seemed efficient and no-nonsense. Cassie sat with her hands politely folded in her lap. This might be the most important appointment of her entire life. The best Christmas present she'd ever get—even if it was from herself. A husband for Christmas. Hmm…

The great Dr. Simon Dodson kept her waiting a full thirty minutes. Cassie knew because she glanced at her watch every five minutes, crossed and uncrossed her legs and flipped through three magazines. By then, she'd grown impatient and irritable and had started to wonder if she'd made a mistake—or, worse, fallen for a scam. She wasn't accustomed to being ignored. She had better things to do than sit in a waiting room on what might turn out to be a fool's errand, a complete waste of time. She trusted that wasn't the case; still, the longer she waited, the less hope she had.

A buzzer made her jump. Ms. Snelling got smoothly to her feet, obviously used to such a peremptory summons. "Dr. Dodson will see you now," she said. She motioned toward the massive double doors that led into his office.

Cassie walked inside and her gaze went instantly to the man standing behind the large desk. The Internet research she'd done hadn't included any photos, so she hadn't been sure what to expect—but not someone relatively young with shockingly good looks. He was easily six-two and loomed above her.

"Ms. Beaumont?"

"That would be me," she said, straining to sound cool and collected.

"Please don't sit down."

"Uh…" The door closed behind her.

"Walk to the far side of my office and then walk back."

Cassie paused, which apparently he didn't like because he gestured for her to comply.

"Do I need to say, 'Mother, may I?'" she asked.

He didn't so much as crack a smile. "That won't be necessary."

"Okay." She did as he requested and felt his eyes burning into her with every step she took.

"You could stand to lose five pounds."

"I beg your pardon?" What a jerk!

"You heard me and you agree with me, only I doubt you'd admit it."

Okay, maybe she *could* shed a few pounds, but her figure looked fine the way it was.

He continued to study her and his frown deepened. "That color doesn't flatter you."

How dare he! "I happen to like navy blue." This was her favorite suit and she'd purchased it at a closeout sale for seventy percent off.

He frowned. "Pale blue would be better." He came out from behind his desk and walked around her. "You should let your hair grow, as well. That style is becoming but you need more length."

"I'm glad you think there's *something* attractive about me."

"I didn't say that."

This man was too much! Cassie was tempted to turn

around and leave. She might have, only she decided to see how many other ways he could find to insult her. It was becoming a game to her.

"Sit," he said.

"Please?" Someone needed to teach this man some manners.

"Sit," he repeated, more loudly this time.

"Sit, *please,*" she returned pointedly.

A flicker of a smile showed in his dark brown eyes. "All right, sit, *please.*"

"Don't mind if I do," she said pleasantly, taking the chair across from his desk.

After a moment he said, "I've read your application." He sat down across from her, reached for the papers and leafed through them. "Tell me about your father."

"Why are you asking about him?"

He lifted his shoulder in a nonchalant shrug. "It's my experience that most women want to marry a man just like their father."

"Not me. Pete's a poor excuse for a father. I want as little to do with him as possible."

Simon immediately made a lengthy notation on a pad in front of him.

Cassie moved to the edge of the cushion. "What did you write?"

Simon looked up, a frown darkening his face. Clearly she'd offended him. She could only suppose he wasn't accustomed to anyone questioning his actions. "What did you say?" he said frostily.

"I asked if you'd tell me what you wrote down." She pointed at his notepad. "It was about me and my nonrelationship with my father, wasn't it?"

He flattened his hands on the desk. "These are my notes. I don't share them with clients."

The urge to stand and simply walk out the door was nearly overwhelming. Gritting her teeth, she said, "Has anyone ever told you you're rude?"

He grinned as if the comment pleased him. "As a matter of fact, yes. Several people have taken delight in revealing their opinions." He shook his head. "It has more to do with them and their hurt feelings than with me."

"What others think doesn't bother you?"

He gave a bored sigh. "Not particularly. Why should it? Now listen, Ms...." He glanced down at the application in an apparent effort to locate her name.

"Beaumont," she supplied.

"Ms. Beaumont," he said impatiently. "This is my office and *I* ask the questions here. Kindly refrain from interrupting me."

She leaned back in the chair. "By all means, ask away." She waved in his direction as though granting him permission to continue.

He narrowed his eyes. "In as few words as possible, explain to me why you aren't married."

That was easy enough to answer. She thought of what Angie had said a few days earlier. "I've been told my standards are too high."

He raised his eyes from the page, his expression startled.

"I guess you could say I'm choosy," she amended. "I'm looking for a perfect match. Someone who's just right—for me. The perfect man, the perfect marriage…and," she added, almost in a whisper, "the perfect Christmas."

He didn't respond. "You're how old?" he asked, instead. He ran his finger down the application.

"Thirty-four. How old are you?"

He exhaled. "As I requested earlier, kindly refrain from asking questions. My age is not your concern."

"Answer me one question, and then I promise not to ask anything else."

He glared at her.

"Just one," she cajoled. "You can't imagine how uncomfortable it is to sit here and have you scrutinize me. It's only fair that I should know something about you."

Sighing, he set the application aside, but before he could speak, she blurted out, "Are you married?"

His eyebrows arched. "*That's* your one question?"

"Yes, and it's important."

"Why is that?"

"Well, first, if you haven't been able to find yourself a wife, what qualifies you to find me a husband?"

"All I will say is that a doctor doesn't need to have a disease in order to cure it. I'm good at what I do. If I wasn't, I wouldn't be willing to offer a refund if I'm unsuccessful in locating a husband for you."

"Are you always so stiff and formal—as if your underwear's been starched?"

He stood abruptly. "I believe that will be all for this afternoon."

"You're sending me away?" She blinked, disappointed. Cassie was just starting to enjoy this. His typical clients were probably more respectful, if not downright obsequious.

"This interview is over."

"Did I pass?" She'd rather know now than be left hanging. She guessed not. She wouldn't be surprised if he didn't take her on. And yet, disagreeable though he was, Simon Dodson intrigued her.

He hesitated. "I'll be in touch later this week."

This was a line Cassie had heard before. "In other words, don't call me, I'll call you."

"Precisely."

Cassie recognized her marching orders. She bent down for her purse and reluctantly stood.

As she drove back to her condo, she tried to make sense of her short interview. On her way up, she collected her mail and noticed once again that the Tuesday paper was missing. Mrs. Mullinex, no doubt.

She ran for the elevator and saw Mr. Oliver, who lived on the same floor, standing inside. Looking her right in the eye, he let the doors close instead of holding them for her. This wasn't the first time, either. He was an unsociable man; the most she'd been able to coax out of him was a muffled greeting, as if he begrudged every word he was forced to speak.

When she got to her condo, she saw that she had company.

"Shawn!" Her brother had made himself at home and was wolfing down a sandwich while standing over her kitchen sink.

"Hey, it's about time you got home. Where were you?"

Rather than explain, Cassie walked over and hugged her big brother. "I had an appointment. How long are you here?" she asked.

"Two days, maybe three."

Shawn often had only a few days' rest before he flew to some other town where another commission awaited him. She knew he was headed to Phoenix, Arizona, next. He had his own home in Portland, but every now and then he dropped in on her. In an effort to encourage his visits, she'd given him a key to her condo.

"I take it you're hungry."

"Starved."

"Let me fix you something decent." Cassie checked the contents of her refrigerator, then reached for a frying pan. She loved to cook and had a small repertoire of favorite dishes. This was one. "How does taco salad sound?"

"Like ambrosia from the gods." He sat on the stool and watched her move about the compact kitchen. "You're going to make some man a wonderful wife."

She whirled around to face him. "Funny you should say that."

Shawn went still. "You've met someone?"

"I would've told you!" They weren't in the habit of keeping secrets from each other. "My appointment this afternoon was with a professional matchmaker."

Her brother's head went back as if the announcement had shocked him. "Get out of here! A matchmaker?"

"I had my first appointment with the great and mighty Dr. Simon Dodson."

"How'd it go?"

Cassie set the onion on the chopping board and paused. "I'm not sure. Simon's pretty rude, but apparently he knows his stuff."

"Simon, is it?"

In her mind it was. "Yeah. He's not a medical doctor, even though he has a bunch of letters behind his name."

Her brother looked unconvinced. "You checked his references?"

"I did. I spoke with two couples who met through him. I was warned in advance that he isn't the most likeable fellow on the face of the earth, but they say he has this gift."

"How'd you hear about him?"

"Through Angie."

"Angie?" Her brother appeared as astonished by this as Cassie had been. "I wouldn't think she'd need a matchmaker. Did she go to him?"

Cassie nodded.

"When?"

"A little while ago. She didn't really say. What I don't get is why Simon rejected her."

"That's crazy! Angie's great."

"And I'm not?" she asked, her hand on her hip.

Shawn chuckled. "I'm staying as far away from that question as I can. What did the matchmaker say? If he rejected Angie, then what about you?"

That was the thirty-thousand-dollar question. "I don't know if Simon will accept me as a client or not. He said he'd phone, but..." The rest of her sentence was drowned out by loud rap music coming from the condo to the right of hers.

"Good grief, what's that?" Shawn covered his ears.

"My new neighbor," Cassie shouted back. She walked over to the kitchen wall and banged hard three times. Within half a minute, the music had been turned down to a more respectable volume.

"Jalapeño?" she asked next, hardly missing a beat.

"Might as well. My life could do with a bit of spicing up."

"Mine, too."

"So tell me more about this matchmaker. Do you like him?"

Cassie began tearing lettuce industriously. "The truth is, I don't. He's arrogant, snooty and definitely not my type. I'm not his, either. Not that it matters... But he doesn't like to be questioned or challenged. I could tell I irritated him."

"You heard he's successful, though, right?"

"Yeah." Until that moment, Cassie hadn't realized how much she hoped Simon would agree to work with her. "I don't know if he's ready for someone like me."

"What do you mean?"

She waved a lettuce leaf in his direction. "Like I said, I questioned his actions and his decisions. He didn't like it."

"I wonder why he rejected Angie," Shawn mused. "I mean, she's not annoying or—"

"Hey, stop right there."

Shawn laughed and leaned his elbows on the counter

where he sat. "Who's that picture of on the fridge?" he asked.

Although she didn't need to turn and look, Cassie did. She tensed slightly as she stared at the photograph of Jill and Tom and their perfect Christmas. "That, brother dearest, is my inspiration."

Chapter 3

A few minutes later, Cassie reached for her phone on impulse and dialed Angie's number.

"Hello? Oh, Cassie, I was hoping you'd call. How'd the appointment go?"

"Do you like taco salad?" Cassie asked rather than answering.

"Is there any food group I don't like?" Her friend had a smile in her voice.

"Silly question. Come join us."

"Us?"

"Yes, Shawn stopped by. I'm making a taco salad and

if you have fresh tomatoes bring one. If not, we'll do without."

"Shawn's there? Your brother?"

"That's what I just said. Are you coming or not?"

"I'm on my way, and I've got a tomato," Angie said, "but when I get there, I want details about the meeting with Dr. Dodson."

Shawn grabbed an orange from her fruit bowl and tossed it in the air, juggling it with an apple and doing a poor job. The orange hit the floor and rolled into the living room. "I'm glad you invited Angie. How's she doing?"

"You know Angie. She's always in a good mood."

Her brother retrieved the orange. "Well…it'll be nice to see her again."

Cassie nodded absently as she began to sauté the ground beef.

By the time Angie arrived, Cassie had the hamburger with taco sauce simmering together. The salad fixings were in a large bowl, awaiting Angie's tomato. Shawn was grating the cheese.

Angie brightened the moment she walked into the room. "Shawn, it's great to see you."

"You, too." He set the cheese down long enough to give her a brief hug. Cassie always forgot how tiny her friend was until Angie stood next to her brother, who was well over six feet.

While Cassie got out the bag of tortilla chips and assembled the rest of the salad, Angie set the table and Shawn filled their water glasses. "Sorry I don't have any sangria," Cassie said as she carried the large wooden bowl to the table. Smaller bowls of meat, cheese and chips followed.

"This looks wonderful," Angie told her.

"Allow me." Shawn pulled out Angie's chair. Then he hurried around to the other side of the table to do the same for Cassie.

"Since when have you acquired gentlemanly manners?" Cassie asked.

Jokingly Shawn checked his watch. "About five minutes ago."

"Perfect timing."

"I'm dying to hear how everything went this afternoon," Angie said, her fork poised over the salad. "How was the meeting with…Dr. Dodson?" She glanced toward Shawn as if she wasn't sure she should say any more.

"It's okay." Cassie nodded. "He knows all about it."

Shawn rolled his eyes. "Personally I think she's nuts. So, what's the story with you and this matchmaker?"

Angie ignored the question and returned her attention to Cassie. "Don't keep me in suspense. What was your impression when you met him?"

"He's abrupt and ill-mannered, don't you agree?"

"That's putting it mildly." She turned to Shawn. "He rejected me. I didn't make it past the initial interview. I'll admit it was a blow to my ego but I felt I had to tell Cassie about him."

"I can't believe he'd reject you." Shawn looked genuinely outraged on Angie's behalf. "I don't understand why either of you would have any interest in someone who seems to enjoy insulting you."

"Why?" Cassie answered. "We're getting desperate, that's why. It's not easy to meet decent men, you know!"

"Not at our age," Angie added.

"See that picture of Jill and Tom?" Cassie said, pointing to her refrigerator. "She has the perfect life, the perfect family and is about to have the perfect Christmas. I want all that."

"Me, too," Angie murmured fervently. "And so far I haven't even come close."

Shawn blinked. "You two are actually serious?"

"Serious enough to pay thirty thousand bucks to find the right man."

Shawn's eyebrows shot up. "*How* much?"

Cassie didn't feel like repeating it. "You heard me."

Shaking his head, Shawn muttered something about being in the wrong business.

Angie sighed. "It's a ridiculous amount of money, I know, but from what I understand, it's worth every penny—if you're accepted, that is. Now, Cassie, tell me about your meeting with Dr. Dodson."

Mentally reviewing the appointment, Cassie suffered more than a few doubts. "I don't think I went over well."

"But you have a second appointment, right?"

"Supposedly." Cassie shrugged. "He said he'd call…."

"Cassie, that's great! Dr. Dodson read my application, took one look at me and said he didn't have anyone who'd suit me."

That wasn't precisely what Angie had told her earlier. Simon had apparently said she already held feelings for someone. If that *was* the case, Cassie didn't have any idea who it might be. She wished she'd questioned her further, but at the time she'd been too interested in hearing about this matchmaker and now didn't seem appropriate. Especially since Angie was obviously reluctant to talk about her own situation. The man in question must've been someone she'd met years ago, which was what Angie had implied. It certainly wasn't anyone Cassie knew, and they'd worked together for six years.

"Tell us what he said," Angie urged.

"Simon was pretty rude," Cassie said between bites of her salad. She added another layer of crushed tortilla chips to the lettuce.

"How?" Shawn asked. "I want specifics."

"Well, he didn't seem to like a single thing about me. Not my body type, not my choice of clothes or the color of my suit."

"I love that suit!" Angie cried.

"I did, too," Cassie said, immediately noting that she'd used the past tense. Hard as it was to admit, he was right about that. She would've preferred it in a soft robin's-egg blue, but the only available color had been navy.

"Didn't he have *anything* nice to say?" Angie asked.

"Well...he did mention that my hairstyle suited me but it needed more length. That was as close to a compliment as he got."

"But you made it past the first interview," Angie said again, as though Cassie had managed a feat of unparalleled skill.

"What I don't understand," Shawn said, pushing back in his chair, "is why you'd allow this man to insult you. I mean, everything he said was just a matter of opinion. *His* opinion." He raised both hands as the women started to protest. "Okay, I understand you're feeling desperate—to quote you—but I don't get it."

Cassie and Angie shared a look.

"I think it's the promise," Cassie said.

"The promise," Shawn repeated. "What promise?"

Angie leaned forward, folding her arms on the table. "Dr. Dodson guarantees that he'll find you a match."

"Someone who'll be a perfect match..."

"Someone who's as eager to meet us as we are them," Angie explained.

"The thing is," Cassie said, "I can't help wondering if the man of my dreams is actually out there."

"Of course he is," Shawn insisted. "Frankly I think all of this is nonsense. How can anyone *guarantee* that he'll find you a *perfect match?*" Sarcasm dripped from his words. "I can't believe you're willing to pay the guy that much money when you're completely capable of finding yourself a husband."

"Where?" Cassie asked, opening her arms and gesturing widely. "Tell me where he is and I'll send a search party to bag him."

"I'll volunteer," Angie said. "Maybe there'll be an extra man hanging around for me."

"Where?" Shawn ignored their teasing. "There are men, decent men, everywhere. You can meet him at work—" they shook their heads simultaneously "—well, then, at…at the grocery store. Or on the street. Or in a bookstore. Or…"

Angie cocked one finely shaped eyebrow. "Did you hear what I just heard?"

"I did," Cassie confirmed.

"What?" Shawn looked from one woman to the other.

"You used the word *meet,*" Cassie told him.

"Not marry," Angie said.

"Now, just a minute—" Shawn started to speak but Cassie cut him off.

"You're a prime example of what we're talking about."

"Me?" Shawn placed a hand over his heart. "I'm too

busy for a wife and family. I'm constantly on the road. That's no life for kids."

"You don't feel the need for companionship, then?" Angie asked.

"Not really."

"Men don't," Cassie complained. "They don't know they're miserable until we tell them."

"So I'm miserable now?" Shawn laughed as if she'd made a joke. "Too bad I've never noticed."

Cassie wasn't about to argue with him. "Men aren't on the same timetable women are, and when they finally wake up and realize they want the same things we do, *they* can still father children."

"A woman has biological limitations," Angie said, "if she wants kids."

Her brother's look sobered. "You two aren't kidding."

"No way," Cassie said. "In fact, we're willing to put up with the criticism and scrutiny of someone like Simon Dodson in the hope of finding a good man we can share our lives with."

Shawn grew thoughtful. "I don't understand why he'd reject *you,* Angie. It seems to me you'd be an ideal candidate."

"Well, he did, and it's his prerogative," she said briskly.

Then she smiled at Cassie. "I can hardly wait until you have your next appointment."

"Now, just a minute," Shawn said again. "You should've asked me to set you up before you went to all this trouble."

Cassie's eyes widened. "You have someone you want me to meet?"

"Well, sure. I know a dozen eligible men. I could've introduced you."

Cassie glanced at Angie. "He only thinks to mention this now?"

Angie frowned. "Do you really trust your brother to find you a husband?"

Cassie shook her head. "My idea of what I want and what he has to offer might be worlds apart."

"Hey, you two," Shawn said, breaking into their conversation. "I'm sitting right here. If you have any doubts, you can address them to me directly and not to each other."

"Okay," Cassie said. "Tell me about one such man."

"All right." He appeared to be deep in thought.

"I don't think he can scrounge up even one," Cassie whispered, raising her eyebrows.

"Give me a minute, would you," he snapped.

"Notice how testy he gets when challenged."

Her brother silenced her with a look.

"There's Riley," he declared triumphantly. He beamed a smile at Angie and then Cassie.

"I've always liked the name Riley," Angie said.

"Riley." Cassie threw back her head. "You're joking!"

"What's wrong with Riley?" Angie wanted to know.

"He's an artist friend of Shawn's. He's got two ex-wives, a gambling problem and he drinks too much. You're scraping the bottom of the frying pan if you're suggesting either of us should marry *Riley.*"

"He's reformed."

"Yeah, right. And when did this happen?"

Shawn seemed unsure. "Not too long ago. He said he's through messing up his life. What he needs now is a good woman."

Cassie exhaled slowly. "Tell him to talk to one of his ex-wives, then."

"Sorry," Angie said, "I'm not interested, either."

"You're going to have to try harder than that," Cassie informed her brother.

"What about Larry Upjohn? You couldn't meet a nicer guy if you tried."

"Do you know Larry?" Angie asked her.

Cassie nodded. "He's Shawn's CPA and in a word… *b-o-r-i-n-g.*"

"You didn't say you were looking for a stand-up comic," Shawn said, obviously annoyed.

"Call me superficial, but I don't want to date a man who wears knee-high socks with his sandals and a pocket protector in his pajamas."

"A little personality would be helpful," Angie said in a defeated voice. "As you can tell, it's not as easy as it seems."

"Warren!" Shawn's face lit up. "What about Warren?"

Once more Angie turned to Cassie.

She nodded, but without enthusiasm. "Warren's a…possibility."

"What's wrong with Warren?" Shawn cried.

Cassie shrugged. "Nothing really. He just doesn't ring my bells. He might Angie's, though."

Shawn leaned back, throwing out his arms in an expansive gesture. "I can introduce you, if you like."

"Tell me about him first," Angie said.

"He's Shawn's agent," Cassie explained. "He's a nice guy."

"Nice isn't a word I'd use to describe Warren," Shawn commented. "He's a tough negotiator."

"But a real kitten on the inside," Cassie said. "He's also divorced. Recently, if I remember."

"He and Clare split last year. I don't know many guys your age who aren't divorced."

"That's reassuring," Cassie muttered. Warren was the best of the rather shallow pool of Shawn's male friends and acquaintances. Shallow pools, as everyone knew, were usually the slimiest, too. This was exactly why she'd decided on the matchmaker.

"Warren's got a couple of kids. His wife has custody."

"Thanks, big brother, but I'll stick with Dr. Dodson."

"I appreciate the suggestion," Angie said, "but I'll pass on Warren, too."

"If I think of anyone else, I'll give you a call."

"You do that," Cassie said, although she didn't expect he would. "On second thought, phone Angie."

Chapter 4

Simon says: I can find the right mate for everyone. Even you!

Simon kept Cassie waiting forty-five minutes on her next visit. His assistant, Ms. Snelling, had called the day after her first appointment. It was now Friday. Since she'd been on pins and needles for three whole days, an additional forty-five minutes didn't bother her. Today would be when he'd announce whether he'd found her a match.

She couldn't figure out how, based on their brief conversation, Simon would be able to match her up with the perfect man. Maybe, as Angie said, it really was all about his ability as a psychologist, his scientific study of her lengthy questionnaire.

For three nights now, she'd been like a kid at Christmas—only instead of sugar plums dancing around in her head she saw men's faces. Men who were enthralled with her. Men who'd go through the same insulting rigmarole she had for the chance to meet her. Men who were just as eager for the very things she wanted—a home and family, security, a sense of belonging and a lifetime filled with love. And one of those men would be her perfect match.

"Dr. Dodson will see you now," Ms. Snelling said in the same crisp tone she'd used on Cassie's first visit.

Cassie bounded up from the chair as though she'd been ejected. Despite her eagerness, she tried to move slowly and calmly. When she entered his office, she found Simon sitting at his desk.

Without looking up, he gestured for her to sit, too.

Cassie did, perching on the very edge. She didn't expect an apology for being kept waiting and wasn't disappointed. When Simon eventually looked up, she noticed streaks of gray in his hair that had escaped her notice previously.

"What are your plans for Christmas?" he asked.

Of all the things Cassie had expected him to say, this wasn't it. "Ah…I'm not sure yet."

"Family plans?"

"Not really." She hadn't talked to her brother yet. Her mother and stepfather lived in Hawaii and it was unlikely that they'd fly in for the holidays. Her father…well, she hadn't spent Christmas with him since she was five or six. "There's just Shawn and me."

"And Shawn is?"

"My brother. It's on the questionnaire. He's—"

"Ah, yes," Simon broke in. "What did you do last Christmas?"

"Well, let me see…" She tried to remember where she'd been and with whom. Was it last year that Angie—

"This shouldn't be so difficult," he said.

"It was eleven months ago," she snapped. His attitude irritated her. "As I recall, Shawn and I went out to eat. Angie, a friend of mine, was supposed to join us but at the last minute she couldn't and we—"

"Yes, yes," he said, interrupting her again.

"And what exactly were *you* doing?" she demanded.

His eyes widened. "I beg your pardon?"

"Where were you last Christmas?"

"As I indicated during our previous session, I'm the one asking the questions."

Cassie made an effort to hold her temper. "I guess that slipped my mind. But I was allowed one question then, so I assume that's the case today, and I'm asking it now." She took a deep—and necessary—breath. "Where were *you* last Christmas?"

He exhaled slowly. "Right here in Seattle."

"With friends and loved ones?"

"That's more than one question." He looked pointedly in her direction. "Shall we continue or not? The choice is yours."

Knowing she was fighting a losing battle, Cassie tried to regain her equilibrium. "Yes, let's continue, although I don't understand what last Christmas has to do with anything."

"That's not your concern."

"Are you always this dictatorial?" She realized she was asking yet another question, but she couldn't stop herself.

"I am when I feel I can find the right match for a client. An exasperating one, I might add."

"Really?" That was worth all the insults he could issue, Cassie decided. She slid so far to the edge of the chair that she was in danger of falling onto the carpet. "You actually have someone in mind?"

"I do." This was said in a clipped, businesslike way.

She waited, but he wasn't any more forthcoming than that.

"Before I introduce you, there are a few matters we need to attend to."

"Fine." Her heart felt as if it had moved into her throat.

"My fee is thirty thousand dollars."

"Yes, I know... That's a lot of money."

Simon glanced up. "I thought you were aware of my fee. If you can't afford me, then I suggest you leave now and save us both a lot of time and trouble."

The money was safely tucked in Cassie's savings account. "I put it aside for a wedding, but obviously there won't be one without a groom. I'm willing to make the investment."

"Good. Then I'll introduce you to John."

"His name is John?" John was a solid name, implying that he was a solid man; she liked him already.

"Before I introduce you—"

"There's a money-back guarantee, right?"

"I'll explain that in a moment."

"Okay, sorry, I didn't mean to interrupt." She wanted to capture every single detail of this meeting so she could repeat it all to Angie.

"I have three tasks I want you to complete first."

"Excuse me?" She wondered if she'd misheard him. Cassie was waiting to hear about her perfect mate, and he was talking about *tasks?* What was this, homework?

"These are qualifying tasks," he was saying. "I need to be sure you're the woman for John."

"But…no one said anything about needing to qualify."

He ignored her outburst. "Once you've fulfilled these three *simple* tasks, I will introduce you to John. The choice is easy—do what I ask and meet the man of your dreams or keep your money and walk away now." He sat back in his chair and clasped his hands, clearly regarding this as a take-it-or-leave-it proposition.

Cassie's head reeled. "Do you ask this of all your clients?" she cried, almost positive he didn't. Her nerves were quickly fraying.

"How often do I need to tell you? I'm not in the habit

of answering questions." He paused and looked her straight in the eye. "However, I'll admit that I don't ask this of every client. Only certain ones."

"What made me so lucky?"

"Your motives. You expect to find the perfect husband, the perfect marriage and the perfect Christmas, correct?"

She remembered having said as much. She nodded.

"You're asking for the impossible."

"But…isn't that what you promised?"

"No. If you'll examine my Web site, you'll see that I promise the *right* mate. The most suitable spouse. But that's just the beginning. A happy marriage is about much more than the appearance of perfection."

Others had found true love. Jill and Tom had, so why couldn't she? "I can dream, can't I?" she muttered.

"Yes, you can dream as long as your dreams are rooted in reality."

"And you consider it your duty to drag me out of my happy fantasy and into the real world," she said sarcastically.

"What I consider my duty is to match you up with someone who'll spend the rest of his life thinking he's the most fortunate man alive to be with you."

"Oh." She swallowed tightly.

"Do you accept the three tasks or not?"

She hesitated. She needed more information before she agreed to anything. "What are they?"

"I'm not asking you to swim in shark-infested waters, if that's what you're worried about. It's nothing life-threatening."

"I won't have to eat anything disgusting, will I?"

He cringed. "Good grief, no. As I said, these are simple, ordinary tasks. It sounds as if you've been watching too much reality television."

"Actually, I don't. My friend Angie watches that stuff and then tells me about it the next day."

He ignored her explanation and reached for a slip of paper on his desk. "Here's your first task. I need you to volunteer for a four-hour shift as a bell ringer in front of the Southcenter Mall near Kent. Do you know it?"

"I know every mall within a two-hundred-mile radius of Seattle."

"I have no doubt of that."

Really, how difficult could a four-hour shift be? "Sure, that won't be a problem."

"It's the weekend after Thanksgiving."

"Great. The mall will be hopping."

"There's a quota the charity expects you to make, but I don't think you'll have any trouble with that."

"Okay. What's the second task?" The first one didn't seem too hard; the next one was probably along similar lines.

"You said on the application form that you're interested in a man who wants children."

"I am."

"Good. I'm going to give you the opportunity to spend an entire afternoon with the little darlings. You'll be one of Santa's elves for a picture-taking session at the Tacoma Mall."

"An elf?"

"There's a costume. I apologize, but it's one of the requirements."

"Okay, fine, I can be an elf." She didn't like the idea of wearing some silly outfit with tights and pointed shoes but she could cope. "And the final task?"

He reached for another slip of paper. "I also saw on your application that you enjoy cooking."

"I do." And she was pretty good at it if she did say so herself.

"Excellent. For your third task, I want you to cook

Christmas dinner. Turkey, stuffing, mashed potatoes with gravy, salad, vegetables...that sort of thing. Oh, and two different kinds of homemade pie."

"And who's going to be eating this huge meal?"

"Your neighbors."

"Ah." She raised her index finger in protest. "I don't have the friendliest neighbors...."

"Invite them, anyway."

"And who's going to check up to see if I've completed these tasks?" she asked. She suspected Simon hadn't thought this completely through.

"I'll be checking in on you during the first two tasks."

"You might as well come to Christmas dinner, then. Can I invite my brother and best friend, too?"

"Of course," he said, but he didn't respond to her admittedly reluctant invitation.

"Can they bring a contribution?" She was thinking Shawn could scrounge up a cooked turkey somewhere and even Angie could manage stuffing out of a box.

"No, you will be providing the entire meal."

Cassie was afraid of that.

"Now that you know the tasks, do you feel you can handle them?"

"I guess so—but what exactly is the point?"

He smiled—a glimmer of a smile. "Each task will tell me something about you. Something important. However, you don't seem very confident. Can you or can't you? A yes or no will suffice."

Lifting her hand to her brow she saluted him smartly. "Aye, aye, sir."

Her gesture failed to amuse him, but he did relax somewhat. "Now that we've squared away that portion of our discussion, it's time to finalize the paperwork."

"All right. Oh—do I get to ask three things of you—small, easy-to-perform tasks?"

He sent her a withering look.

"Obviously I don't," she said under her breath.

"Let's make this clear," he said with exaggerated patience. "*You're* the one who sought me out. You came to me because of your desire for a husband and a family. I don't advertise. I didn't ask you to step into this office. You came of your own free will."

"I did," she concurred.

"Then we play this by my rules."

She resisted rolling her eyes for fear he'd demand she leave. "Rules," she repeated softly. "Is this a game to you?"

"No, this is life, yours and John's. He's a good man who wants the same things you do."

"Okay, I accept your rules."

"Thank you."

"Can I at least see his photograph?"

"No. You will meet when it's time. There will be no information exchanged before that official meeting."

Cassie didn't like it, but she didn't have any alternative. She nodded.

Simon opened a side drawer and withdrew a contract. "I advise you to have your attorney look this over before you sign it. This is a standard contract, stating what you can expect for your thirty thousand dollars."

"What if John and I don't gel? If we aren't a good fit?"

"That occasionally happens and it's a fair question. Your money will be refunded to both of you in full."

"In that case, will you introduce me to another potential mate?"

"No."

"No. No?"

"This is a one-shot deal."

"One-shot?" That sounded risky.

"If I offered choices, my clients would be wondering

who else might be available. When I pick a mate for you, it's the best match I can find, someone I believe will complement your strengths, share your values and fulfill your desires—within reasonable parameters."

"And your success rate is?"

"High. I don't accept a client unless I'm confident I have the right person for him or her. It's as simple as that."

Cassie stared down at the contract. She'd feel better if she liked Simon more. The man was rude, arrogant and short-tempered.

It was as if he'd read her thoughts. "You don't need to like me, Cassie," he said. "In fact, it's preferable that you don't."

"Really?"

"Yes, really," he returned. "The last thing I want or need is for a client to fall in love with me. It only complicates matters, and I don't like unnecessary complications. Understood?"

"Now who's dreaming?"

A smile came and went. A smile that charmed her despite everything he'd said and done.

Chapter 5

Simon says: Maybe money can't buy love—but it can get you practically everything else.

On the Saturday morning after Thanksgiving, which she'd spent with Angie and her family, Cassie headed for Southcenter Mall. This was the venue for her first task and she was eager to prove herself to Simon, obviously a curmudgeon. Spending four hours soliciting money for charity couldn't possibly be that difficult.

Since she'd be standing outside, Cassie dressed in wool pants and a hand-knit sweater over her long-sleeved blouse. Between the shirt and sweater, she could barely get her arms inside the sleeves of her coat. She added a hat, gloves and a scarf, dressing for the cold. When she met her one true love, she wanted to make sure she didn't have a runny nose and a sore throat.

Cassie showed up at the mall at the required time and met the other charity bell ringers. Standing with her colleagues, she glanced around. Some were being paid and frankly she thought they looked kind of shifty. Others, like her, were volunteers.

"Smile and greet everyone," the leader instructed. "Be friendly even if someone walks past you."

Filled with enthusiasm, Cassie could hardly wait to be assigned her post.

"Make eye contact" was the second bit of advice. "And ring that bell. Remind shoppers of those less fortunate."

"Got it," Cassie said aloud.

"This is one of the busiest shopping weekends of the year, so you shouldn't have any problem making your quota."

In the back of her mind, she recalled Simon's casually mentioning something about collecting a certain dollar amount and the way he'd made light of it. The recommended donation amount turned out to be $60 an hour. That was a dollar a minute! How was she supposed to know how much money she'd collected when the red pot was securely locked? It wasn't as if she could pry the lid off and count the cash.

"Are we ready?" their helpful leader called out.

Cassie's shout blended in with the others'. "Ready!"

One by one, they received their assignments. Cassie was told to stand in front of the Target store, which had an outside entrance. With bell in hand, she headed toward her designated post. This wasn't so bad. Not only was she helping the underprivileged but she was moving toward the man of her dreams.

She waited eagerly as a couple walked up. Smiling sweetly, she jerked her hand several times in succession, making the bell jangle. "Merry Christmas," she greeted them.

The couple avoided eye contact and entered the store via the door farthest from Cassie.

Their lack of generosity—and appreciation for her efforts—didn't faze her.

Not much later, a grandmotherly type approached her. "Do you have change for a five?" the woman asked.

"Sorry, we can't make change."

"Oh, dear," she said regretfully, "then perhaps I can give you something on my way out."

"Don't worry," Cassie said cheerfully, "I'll be here."

In her first thirty minutes, Cassie estimated that she'd collected less than five dollars, which wasn't even close to her hourly goal. She stomped her feet to ward off the cold. In an effort to liven things up a bit, she attempted to ring the tunes of popular Christmas songs.

She gave that up during "Frosty the Snowman" when a teenage boy walked past and reached for his cell phone. He said, "Hello. Hello. Hello," before he realized it was her bell and not his cell. He stopped in front of her and glared.

"Sorry," she said, and gasped when the youth shot her the finger.

"Well, Merry Christmas to you, too." Of all the nerve!

After an hour Angie came by and mercifully handed her a cup of steaming hot coffee.

"God love you," she said, gratefully accepting it.

"How's it going?"

If it'd been Simon rather than Angie, she would have declared that this was the most wonderful, rewarding experience of her life. With Angie she felt compelled to tell the truth. "I can't feel my nose."

"Can I get you anything else?" her friend asked, her expression concerned.

"Put some money in the pot. I'm nowhere near my quota."

"Oh, sure." Angie put in a hefty donation.

"Thank you."

"Do you want me to stand in for you? You look like you could use a break."

"No way." Simon Dodson was sure to find out about it and consider her unworthy of John. Cassie wasn't willing to risk that.

"You have a donation quota?"

Cassie nodded. "I bet that guy at the other entrance isn't having this problem," she muttered. Her breath made small whiffs of fog. Her nose wasn't the only body part in danger of frostbite. Even the knit cap wasn't enough to completely protect her ears. She'd swear those weren't earrings dangling from her lobes, but tiny icicles.

"I'll come and see you again later," Angie promised.

"Great, and thanks for the coffee." Cassie wondered

whether anyone would notice if she stuck her nose in the hot liquid.

Angie disappeared inside the mall and Cassie rang her bell with renewed enthusiasm. It helped to remember that in less than three hours she would have completed one of the tasks that would bring her closer to meeting John.

In retrospect she wished she'd pushed Simon to show her John's photograph. Then again, she didn't want any predetermined impressions of him. He was already bigger than life in her mind. She pictured him at the head of a boardroom table or the helm of a sailboat. Or…

Suddenly, she noticed the scruffily dressed middle-aged man standing in front of her. He looked like he belonged to a motorcycle gang. He had on a worn leather jacket that barely zipped up over his protruding belly and a bandanna around his head. His hair, long and greasy and tied in a ponytail, reached to the middle of his back. He made a beeline for Cassie as if destiny had called him to her side.

Her bell ringing became a whole lot less enthusiastic.

He looked her slowly up and down. Then he smiled as if to say her waiting days were over; *he* had arrived. "Hello, there, pretty lady."

Cassie managed a weak smile in return. "Happy holidays." This guy didn't strike her as the charitable type.

"I bet you're real cold standing out here all by yourself."

She didn't respond but his gaze lingered on her, which gave her a decidedly uncomfortable feeling.

"I could find ways to keep us both warm."

"Ah...actually I'm warm as toast," she said. An outright lie. She hoped he didn't notice that, by this time, her nose was probably blue.

A mother and daughter scurried past her. Cassie thrust out her arm and rang the bell as if sounding an alarm during the great San Francisco fire. When the pair resolutely ignored her, she rang the bell using both hands. Still they walked past. In fact, it seemed to Cassie that they went out of their way to avoid her. In other words, she was on her own with the biker.

"We'd be grateful for a donation," she told him.

"I was thinking you could give me one."

"Me? What could I possibly give you?" As soon as she asked the question, Cassie realized her mistake. "Forget I asked that," she said.

"What are you doing after this stint?" he asked.

Cassie could hardly believe this was happening and let her bell-holding hand fall to her side. "Are you trying to pick me up?" she asked incredulously. "You're old enough to be my father." She did her best to hide her revulsion.

"Hey, you can't blame a guy for trying."

"Yes, I can. Now kindly move along. You're discouraging donations." She scowled at him, letting him know she didn't appreciate that he was cutting into her hourly quota.

He chuckled as though amused. "You have no idea what you're missing."

Frankly, Cassie was grateful for the escape. She heaved a sigh of relief when he sauntered off. Her one hope was that when he left the mall he'd use a different exit.

As soon as Mr. Easy Rider was gone, donations picked up. Still, as far as she could figure, Cassie wasn't even close to making the recommended quota, despite her cheerful greetings.

Distracted, she didn't notice another man approaching.

"You should be ashamed of yourself," he said angrily.

Taken aback, she blinked, then asked, "I beg your pardon?" Obviously *he* wasn't the one standing in the cold, ringing his heart out, seeking donations for the poor.

"It isn't even December."

"And your point is?" she challenged, which she recognized almost immediately was a mistake. She didn't want to invite an argument, which she'd inadvertently done.

"Christmas is far too commercial."

"Ah…"

"Everyone's got their hand out. I've had it up to here," he said, slicing the air over his head, "with greedy beggars asking for handouts."

"Greedy beggars?" she repeated, growing agitated. "Don't you have any compassion for others? Where's your Christmas spirit?"

"It doesn't come out until December. Look at these shops! Most of them had their Christmas displays up before Halloween. All they're after is the almighty dollar."

"Go complain to them, not me," she urged, hoping to send Scrooge on his way. "And when you do, say hello to Tiny Tim for me."

"Who?"

"Never mind."

"Those greedy shop owners spoil the true meaning of

Christmas. And you're no better than corporate America, stopping people as they're going into the store. Irritating them with that stupid bell."

"I'm not asking you for anything. The bell is to remind shoppers of the less fortunate. I didn't *stop* you—you're the one who came up to me. Furthermore..." She halted midsentence as it occurred to her that this man might be a plant of Simon's, that he'd purposely headed right over to chat with her.

Cassie eyed him warily. "Simon sent you, didn't he?"

"Simon? Who's Simon?"

"This is a test, isn't it?"

"Lady, I don't know what you're talking about."

"You can't fool me! Simon sent you to see how I'd respond. Well, you can tell him I saw through your little charade and it didn't work." She felt downright smug that Simon hadn't outsmarted her.

Scrooge stared at her, wearing a puzzled look. Then his eyes narrowed. "Lady, I suggest you seek counseling."

"Thank you, but I suggest you make an appointment first. You can tell Simon I said that, okay?"

He backed away from her as if he suddenly suspected she carried an infectious disease.

Donations were few and far between, and Cassie glanced toward her counterpart at the other end of the mall with envy. He had more business than he knew what to do with. She, on the other hand, felt like the Little Match Girl. Using her foot, she eased the red kettle ever so slightly toward the department store entrance. She was about halfway between the two when the other charity collector noticed.

Cassie eased her foot away from the pot and gazed in the opposite direction.

"Hey, you!" he shouted, pointing an accusing finger at her. "You stay in your half of the mall and I'll stay in mine."

Playing innocent, Cassie pressed her gloved hand to her chest. "Are you speaking to me?" she called.

"You drag that kettle one step closer, sister, and you'll live to regret it."

Cassie opened her mouth, then closed it. She'd been caught. There was nothing to do but drag the kettle back, one step at a time.

Eventually Cassie returned to her original spot and figured she'd probably lost thirty minutes in this attempt to find more fertile ground. With no option other than to follow her original plan, she continued to greet the shoppers, doing her best to display a cheerful holiday spirit.

A young couple approached from the mall parking lot and Cassie made eye contact with the man. The woman, who carried a cup of takeout coffee, didn't appear to see her, but he looked friendly enough, so Cassie rang the bell with renewed energy. These people seemed like the kind who'd dig deep into their wallets in order to help the less fortunate.

As they neared the store, just as Cassie had hoped, the man reached in his back pocket for his wallet. This was a good sign. Cassie smiled encouragingly.

The woman walked toward the store entrance, while the man paused in front of Cassie and slipped a twenty-dollar bill into the pot.

The woman quickly rejoined her husband. "How much did you put in there?" she demanded.

"Come on, Alicia, it's for charity."

"Charity begins at home. We've been through this, remember? We're on a Christmas budget. We don't have extra money to be giving away."

The man grimaced apologetically.

"It's for a good cause," Cassie reminded the woman.

"As for you," Alicia said menacingly. "I saw the way you were flirting with my husband. You didn't think I noticed, did you?"

Cassie was too stunned to react. "I wasn't—"

"Don't bother denying it. I have eyes. Maybe the two of you are old *friends.*"

"Alicia," the man snapped.

"That's it, we're finished. It's over." In a fit of anger she tossed the cup of coffee at Cassie.

She gasped and leaped back but not in time to avoid having coffee splash the front of her caramel-colored wool coat.

The man looked horrified, whispered something Cassie couldn't hear, then hurried after his wife. "Alicia, Alicia..."

In shock and denial, Cassie stared down at her coat. Some very unladylike comments formed in her mind. However, she didn't express them since that would reflect poorly on the charitable organization. Within minutes she was glad she'd kept her mouth shut. Because, to Cassie's astonishment, donations started to increase dramatically following the incident. She glanced at the other bell ringer, who was scowling at her. He rang his bell louder and harder.

Cassie retaliated with an all-out rendition of "Deck the Halls" and soon had a short line, everyone waiting to drop in donations. She wasn't sure what had changed but clearly there'd been a reversal. Perhaps her bell ringing was superior. Or perhaps that section of the parking lot had filled up. Whatever the cause, she was taking full advantage of it.

Toward the end of her shift, a sweet old lady sidled up to Cassie with a benevolent smile. She stuffed something inside her coat pocket and leaned close to whisper, "Use this to buy yourself a decent coat, dear. You poor thing."

That was it? People thought she was a charity case and had taken pity on her. Too bad the coffee incident had happened at the end of her four hours. Who knew how much she would've collected if it had occurred earlier.

She nearly laughed aloud when she realized one glove was missing. Cassie didn't have a clue when that had disappeared or how.

Precisely four hours into her assignment, when she was about ready to hand in her kettle and bell, she saw Dr. Simon Dodson. He was walking across the parking lot and headed directly toward her. And he was frowning.

Chapter 6

Simon says: The best match for you is the one *I* arrange.

Just as Simon approached, an elderly gentleman stepped up to the pot and inserted a folded bill.

"Thank you and Merry Christmas," Cassie told him cheerfully.

"No, thank *you,*" the old man returned. "You see, I was on a troop train in World War II and your organization met us at the station as we disembarked and handed out doughnuts and coffee. That small kindness meant the world to those of us going off to war. I've never forgotten it."

Cassie hardly knew what to say.

"A lot of us didn't come home from the war, but I'll bet you those of us who did will always remember the friendly smiles and support you gave us. I'm an old man now and I don't have many more years left." He grew teary-eyed as he spoke. "Merry Christmas, young lady," he whispered, gently squeezing her hand, "and thank you again for the sacrifice you're making on behalf of others."

Now it was Cassie who had tears in her eyes. She brushed them aside as Simon came closer. The old man had disappeared inside the mall by the time he arrived.

"How was it?" he asked.

Cassie tried to swallow the lump in her throat. "My grandfather was in the Second World War, too."

"I beg your pardon?"

"That elderly gentleman," she said, sniffling, "the one who was just here. He told me about something that happened when he went off to war and thanked me as if I was the one who'd been kind to him."

"I didn't see any old man."

"You didn't? He was here a minute ago and was...just wonderful." She didn't understand how Simon could have missed him. It was unlikely that he'd have eyes only for her.

"What happened to your coat?" Simon asked, apparently not interested in hearing about the man who had touched her so deeply.

"Oh, that," she said, glancing down. "That was a lucky break. Well, to be honest, it didn't seem like it at the time, but I collected a lot of pity donations as a result."

He didn't ask her to elaborate. "Your shift is over. You can leave now."

"What about my substitute?" Cassie wasn't about to be lured away from her duty station until the next person was firmly in place.

"That would be me," a cheerful middle-aged woman said from behind Simon, the supervisor at her side.

Cassie handed over the bell, and the supervisor took her full kettle and replaced it with an empty one. "Good luck," Cassie told the new bell ringer and meant every word. She nearly added that the woman was going to need it.

"You didn't tell me how your morning went," Simon said. He walked into the mall with her.

Cassie stood just inside the sliding glass doors for a moment, soaking in the blast of warm air. Until now she hadn't fully realized how utterly cold she'd been. Four hours had felt like forever.

"You don't want to know," she said. Her teeth had only now stopped chattering.

"I don't ask questions if I don't want an answer."

"Okay, fine. I misplaced a glove, and my nose lost feeling in the first half hour." She looked at him and muttered, "It's still there, isn't it? My nose, I mean."

"Yes." His mouth twitched, but he didn't admit he was amused.

"My feet feel like blocks of ice. A jealous wife threw coffee on me and some sweet old lady slipped a fifty-dollar bill into my coat pocket because she felt sorry for me. I threw it in the pot," she added righteously.

Simon arched his brows. That apparently was his only comment.

"Furthermore, I recognized your plant."

"My...plant?"

"The man you sent. Okay, so I made that remark about saying hello to Tiny Tim. Oh, and about seeing a shrink. I probably shouldn't have, but I couldn't help it. He was obnoxious. Did you pay him extra for being rude?" she asked. That sounded like something Simon would do.

He eyed her speculatively, but didn't respond one way or the other.

"He told you, didn't he?" Cassie could easily picture Scrooge running to Simon to tattle on her.

As they walked past a Starbucks, Cassie stopped abruptly. "I would kill for a latte," she said and veered back into the store.

Simon followed, and they stood in line together. When they reached the counter, Cassie ordered her vanilla latte, along with two shortbread cookies. It was after two, and she hadn't had lunch yet.

Simon ordered a large black coffee and paid their bill. Although the small area was crowded, a couple left just then and they were able to secure a table.

Cassie sank gratefully into the chair. She crossed her legs, and removed one boot so she could rub feeling back into her toes, pausing occasionally to sip her latte. It tasted like heaven.

"About this, uh, plant you mentioned."

"Oh, him. Not to worry, I caught on fast enough. Well, maybe not as fast as I should have, but it was obvious that you sent him. He didn't try very hard to hide it, either."

"Not *that* obvious," Simon said mildly. "Because I didn't send anyone."

"Oh, come on. There's no need to carry on this charade."

He regarded her sternly. "I am not in the habit of lying."

She studied him—and realized he just might be telling the truth.

"I will repeat myself this once. I did not send anyone to test you."

"Oh." The man with all the complaints had been so unpleasant that it was a natural assumption.

To hide her embarrassment, Cassie tore the cellophane off her cookies and gobbled them both down.

"What did you learn from the experience?" Simon asked.

She rolled her eyes. "You didn't tell me there'd be an exam."

"It's not an exam. I asked a straightforward question."

"Well…" Cassie took a sip of her latte, then removed her other boot. "For one thing, I will never pass someone standing in the cold ringing a bell and not leave a donation. You wouldn't believe how many people simply look the other way."

"But you've ignored a bell ringer now and then, haven't you?"

"Okay, I may have, but I won't again. I don't think I've ever worked harder at anything."

The merest hint of a smile showed in his eyes.

"You find that funny? Why don't *you* stand out in the cold for four hours and see how you like it?"

"I prefer to write a check."

"Of course you would. It's much easier."

"Agreed. That's the point. Anything else?"

"Well, there was the lovely old man." She turned an angry look on Simon. "You must've chased him away."

"Like I said, I didn't notice any old man and I certainly didn't chase one away."

"He was definitely there. He reminded me of my grandfather. Grampa died when I was young, but I remember him so well." She grew introspective. "He was in the war, too. That old man made everything that happened today worthwhile."

She gestured at her stained coat and her stocking feet, then tentatively at her nose. "I think I'm finally thawing out."

"I'm glad to hear it."

He didn't sound glad. In fact, he sounded bored.

"Tell me about John," she urged.

Simon's deep sigh informed her that she was becoming tiresome. "What do you want to know?"

"Something. Anything. Did you assign him three tasks like you did me? What are they?"

"I won't discuss my other clients with you." The way he said it suggested she'd committed a major faux pas.

She forged ahead despite that. "Has John asked about me?"

Another sigh. "I should never have mentioned his name."

"But you did and now I'm curious. Come on, Simon, have a heart. Give me one small detail, one tiny tidbit, about my hero."

He glanced at her coat and, seeing the huge coffee stain, must have taken pity on her. "All right, if you have to know, he's an engineer."

"An engineer?" she repeated slowly.

"Your children will be left-brain geniuses."

"Children." Overwhelmed with excitement she grasped Simon's hand.

"Restrain yourself, please."

"Oh, Simon, loosen up a little, would you?"

He looked at her coldly, as though her comment didn't merit a response.

"Has John asked about me?"

He nodded.

Rubbing her palms together, she blurted out, "And what did you say?" After asking, she quickly changed her mind. "No, don't tell me—I'd rather not know."

"It wasn't unflattering, if that's what you're implying."

This was promising. "Really?"

"Are you looking for compliments, Cassie?"

"No...well, maybe." Then, because she was curious and she couldn't resist, she asked, "Do you like me, Simon?"

He regarded her for a moment, as though carefully weighing his response. "Not particularly. Wait—let me rephrase that. I don't have any feelings for you whatsoever. Except for the appropriate reactions of a professional toward his client, of course."

What would it have cost him to smile and say something nicc? "You really are a dolt."

He stiffened. "I beg your pardon?"

"You heard me. You know, if you smiled more often you might look human. You're supposed to be a psychologist—haven't you heard that a smile is a positive way of interacting?"

"I don't see any reason to—"

"Forget it. You are who you are, and I am who I am."

"That was profound." He seemed to be making fun of her.

Cassie didn't care. Simon was a means to an end, and if he found her a decent man she could love for the rest of her life, then it didn't matter if he liked her or not.

"When can I complete the second task?" she asked, eager to hurry the process along. From the sound of it, John was equally excited about meeting her.

"I'm making the final arrangements next week. I'll be in touch as soon as everything's set."

"Okay." Cassie finished her latte and dabbed at the crumbs left over from her shortbread cookies. "You're not very good at relationships, are you? Personally, I mean, not professionally."

Acting as if she hadn't spoken, Simon shoved back his chair and seemed about to leave. "As I said earlier, I'll be in touch."

"Before you go, I'd like to ask how you came to this line of work."

"You already know I don't answer personal questions. This isn't about me."

"But it is."

"*Au contraire.* You came to me for services rendered. Do you interrogate your dentist about his background—or private life?"

"No, but—"

"You let him do his job and you walk away satisfied when he's finished. It's the same with me, or it should be. I perform a service, nothing more. I'm good at what I do and I enjoy my work."

"Always?"

"Some matches are more difficult than others. Some clients more trying." He looked pointedly in her direction.

"At least you can take comfort from knowing that once I meet John, you won't ever need to see me again."

"Yes, there is that...."

Cassie couldn't help it; she burst out laughing.

Simon seemed genuinely puzzled. "Why is that funny?"

"It wouldn't have been if you hadn't been so honest about it. You'll be happy to get rid of me, won't you?"

He stood and tossed his empty coffee container in the proper receptacle. "You did very well today, Cassie."

For a moment, she thought her ears had deceived her. "Was that a compliment, an actual *compliment,* from the great Dr. Simon Dodson?"

"Not really," he said soberly. "It was a statement of fact. The truth is, I didn't expect you to last all four hours. You surprised me."

"I want to meet John," she told him, disregarding the implied insult in his words.

"So I gathered, and soon you shall."

Ten minutes later, they left Starbucks together and exchanged civil goodbyes.

Cassie could hardly wait to get back to her condo so she could talk to Angie. The minute she'd showered and changed, she reached for the phone and hit speed dial.

After several rings, she was connected to voice mail. That was odd. Angie hadn't said anything about going out—but then it wasn't as if Cassie was her parole officer.

Much later that afternoon she heard from Angie.

"Where were you?" Cassie asked right away.

"Shopping. 'Tis the season, you know?" Her friend seemed to be in high spirits.

"Did you find any bargains?"

"Lots. How'd the morning go?"

"Simon said I surprised him."

"You saw Dr. Dodson?"

"Yeah, he showed up to check on me. We had coffee afterward."

"You and…Dr. Dodson? Simon?"

"What's so odd about that?"

"I don't know," Angie said. "I just can't picture it."

"It wasn't like a date or anything," Cassie insisted. "More of a…debriefing. He said he'd be in touch next week with the details about my next task. I get to be an elf. That *has* to be easier than what I did this morning."

"I wouldn't be so sure of that," Angie warned her.

Chapter 7

Her arms loaded down with groceries, Cassie hurried over to the elevator. "Mr. Oliver, hold that door for me!" she cried frantically, trying not to drop the quart of milk dangling from her index finger.

Mr. Oliver pretended not to hear, and the doors glided shut in her face.

Cassie ground her teeth in frustration. This wasn't the first time Mr. Oliver had purposely let the elevator close as she ran toward it. She'd watched him do the same thing with other residents. Obviously it gave him some kind of thrill. She might have imagined it, but Cassie swore she saw a glimmer of sadistic humor in his eyes as the doors slid closed.

She lowered one bag to the floor and pushed the call button. While she waited, she went to collect her newspaper, only to discover the slot was empty—and it wasn't even Tuesday. Apparently Mrs. Mullinex was now clipping coupons from the Sunday edition, as well.

Perhaps it was time to confront the retired schoolteacher.

Cassie took the elevator up to the fifth floor, brought her groceries to the kitchen, and walked down the hallway to Mrs. Mullinex's unit. Outside her neighbor's door, she rang the bell until she heard footsteps on the other side.

"Hold your horses," Mrs. Mullinex called out.

She answered the door, wearing her housecoat and slippers. Her head was covered in pink curlers and wrapped with a bandanna knotted directly above her forehead. It wasn't a look Cassie saw very often these days—if ever.

"Why, Cassie, how nice of you to stop by," she said pleasantly. "Can I offer you a glass of eggnog?"

"Oh, no, thank you." Cassie made an attempt to be neighborly or at least polite. "Uh, I believe you have my newspaper."

Her neighbor seemed startled, as if the suggestion that she might have taken something not hers was a devastating insult. Mrs. Mullinex raised one hand to her mouth in a gesture of innocence. "Oh, dear, was that *your* paper?"

Cassie held out her hand.

The older woman slowly retrieved the thick weekend edition and reluctantly placed it in Cassie's outstretched hand. "I was wondering, dear, if you wouldn't mind letting me have the section with the *New York Times* crossword puzzle."

Cassie clutched the paper to her chest.

"Only when you're finished with it, of course."

"I happen to enjoy doing the crossword puzzle, Mrs. Mullinex."

"Oh."

Wondering if she'd been a little too inflexible, Cassie returned to her own condo, put away her groceries and made a cup of coffee. She sat down with the paper, prepared to relax. She'd just turned to the middle section, grabbed a pen—doing the crossword puzzle in pen was a matter of pride—when the rap music started next door. The whole room seemed to vibrate. Cassie groaned. There was no question: the fates were conspiring against her.

Getting up from her chair, Cassie pounded her fist against the kitchen wall hard enough to rattle her dishes. She had to repeat the pounding twice before the music was lowered to a tolerable level.

Settled once more, she rested her feet on the ottoman, crossed her ankles and savored the first sip of coffee when her doorbell rang.

"Oh, for the love of heaven," she muttered, tossing down the pen. If it turned out to be one of her annoying neighbors—whom she'd be having dinner with all too soon, according to Simon—she didn't know what she'd say.

To her astonishment, it was her brother, toting a five-foot Christmas tree.

"Shawn, what are you doing here?" Normally she'd be fortunate to see him twice in four months, and this was his second visit to Seattle in as many weeks.

"Are you complaining?"

"Of course not!"

"I come bearing gifts." He thrust the Christmas tree into the room.

"So I noticed."

Shawn grinned. "I thought you could use a bit of Christmas cheer." He stepped into the condo and leaned the tree against the living room wall. "This also seemed like a good excuse to stop by so you could tell me how everything went yesterday."

Had it only been the day before that she'd stood in the cold, soliciting donations? That didn't seem possible, and yet Cassie hadn't stopped thinking about the experience. What remained uppermost in her mind was the time she'd spent with Simon at the coffee shop. He'd been frank, unemotional, honest. She amended that to *brutally* honest. When she'd met him, she'd considered him rude and arrogant, but since then she'd had a change of heart. Simon, she decided, was simply…direct. He said what he felt and didn't moderate his opinions in deference to other people's flimsy egos. She'd never met anyone quite like him.

"Well?" Shawn prodded her.

"Who do you want to hear about first—Mr. Scrooge, who *wasn't* sent by Simon as a test," she added, "or would you rather I told you about the woman who threw coffee at me because she thought I'd flirted with her husband?"

Shawn flopped down on the sofa. "Both, and while you're up, I'll take a cup of that coffee."

"Sure," she said, while she got a mug and filled it to the brim. "You won't believe what he said to me."

"Scrooge?"

"No, Simon. I asked if he liked me and he said 'not particularly.' What's so funny is the fact that—"

"Funny? You thought this was funny?"

"Not at first," she admitted. "The thing with Simon is that he wasn't being intentionally rude. He's the most plainspoken man I've ever encountered."

"Sounds like a bore to me."

"I called him a dolt." She smiled at the memory. "He didn't much like that."

"So he can dish it out, but he can't take it?"

"Well, he certainly isn't used to it."

They chatted for a while, until Shawn eventually said, "I hope you realize that all you've done is talk about Simon. I've yet to hear a word about anyone else."

"Really?" Caught up in her musing, Cassie hadn't noticed.

"I think you might be falling for him."

"For Simon?" The suggestion was ludicrous. "Oh,

hardly! If I'm focusing on him, it's because he's the man who holds the key to my happiness. He's going to introduce me to John—and I have high hopes for John. He's my perfect—oops, *most suitable,* which is what Simon calls it—match."

"Just in time for the perfect—or should I say, *most suitable*—Christmas."

Cassie suspected Shawn was mocking her a little, but she was too hopeful and too happy to care.

All at once he grew serious. "Don't build your expectations too high, Cassie. What if you and this John character don't really connect?"

"But we will. That's the beauty of it. Simon studied our profiles and concluded that we're ideal for each other. I think his success lies in the fact that he can be emotionally detached and even clinical. It's all quite scientific, you know."

"Uh-huh." Shawn nodded wryly.

"Did I mention Simon refuses to talk about himself? That's probably why he's so brilliant at this. He doesn't want to cloud the relationship between him and his clients. His sole focus is on finding the right person for them."

"Seems to me you've got him all figured out."

"I think I just might. Now wipe that smirk off your face," she said. Now that she'd thought seriously about Simon, and she'd been doing that for the past twenty-four hours, it all made a crazy kind of sense.

Simon made sense.

Simply put, he wasn't encumbered with the need to please others. His skill at matchmaking was based on his knowledge of psychology, as he claimed, but he obviously had good instincts, too. His success rate was impressive, and if he honestly felt John-the-engineer would make her a good husband, then Cassie didn't doubt it for an instant.

"He's an engineer," she murmured.

"Simon?"

"No, my match. Simon offered me a crumb of information yesterday."

"An engineer," Shawn echoed. "I guess your kids will be left-brained."

"That's what Simon said," she returned excitedly.

Shawn looked surprised. "You told him about your IQ?"

"No, but it was on the questionnaire." In high school, her high IQ had been an embarrassment rather than an asset. She always used to insist that scoring well on a test didn't make her any different from everyone else. She still felt that way—although it did get her through two chemistry degrees in four years instead of six.

"Mom was always proud of your intelligence," Shawn reminded her.

"It didn't matter to our father, though, did it?" As a child, Cassie had thought it was her fault their father had left the family. Although it made no sense for a seven-year-old to assume that kind of blame, she had. Later, she'd learned this was fairly typical in situations like this. They'd all been devastated, but she'd unconsciously taken on the role of scapegoat.

"Speaking of Dad..."

Cassie already knew what was coming. "He called you?"

Shawn nodded.

"His yearly sojourn into fatherhood! Lucky you. This year it was your turn to receive the great gift of his phone call. What did he have to say?"

"He saw one of my murals and wanted to tell me he was impressed."

Cassie shrugged. "That was nice."

"A surprise, actually."

Cassie knew how long Shawn had waited for any praise

from their father. They rarely discussed him; the subject was still too painful for them both.

"Where was he?" The last she'd heard, he was living aboard his sailboat somewhere in the Caribbean.

"Hawaii."

Cassie chuckled. "Really? Wouldn't it be amusing if he ran into Mom on the streets of Honolulu?"

Shawn shook his head. "She's over him. She forgave him a long time ago."

"Mom's a better woman than I am." Talking about their father depressed her. "Can't we discuss something else? Something more cheerful—like bank foreclosures?"

Shawn snorted. "Very funny."

"I don't know why he bothers," she said.

"I thought we weren't going to discuss Dad."

"Right. Sorry."

Shawn drank the last of his coffee and stood. "I've gotta go."

"You mean you aren't going to stay and help me trim the tree?"

"Can't. I've got an...appointment."

From the gleam in his eyes, this so-called appointment involved a woman. "You've got a date."

"I'm not telling."

It really wasn't fair. Cassie had to pay tens of thousands of dollars to meet men, and her brother had women falling all over him. It must be those piercing blue eyes of his—plus, of course, the fact that he was talented, rich and eligible.

Cassie walked him to the door.

"Are you coming back here tonight?" she asked.

"Nope. I'm taking the red-eye to Phoenix."

"Will I see you at Christmas?"

"Sure. Where else would I go?"

"Call me, okay?"

"Will do. Besides, I want to hear all about Simon."

"John," she corrected. "Simon's the matchmaker."

"Right." That gleam was back in his eyes and Cassie suspected the slip had been intentional.

An hour later, Cassie had the Christmas tree in its stand and set by the window that overlooked the city. The big star above Macy's glowed in the dim light of late afternoon. She dragged her ornaments out from the guest room closet and decided to give Angie a call. Trimming a tree all alone wasn't any fun.

Her friend answered immediately. "Come on over,"

Cassie invited her. "Shawn stopped by to drop off a Christmas tree and then abandoned me to decorate it by myself. I've got hot apple cider and popcorn popping in the microwave."

"Oh, Cassie, I'd love to but I can't."

"Are you off shopping again?"

"No, I'm meeting an old friend. Sort of a last-minute thing. You could join us if you want."

"Anyone I know?"

"Um, not really."

"Oh, well, I've got an appointment with a box of ornaments, a bowl of popcorn and the DVD of *The Bishop's Wife.*"

Angie sounded regretful. "I hate the thought of you trimming the tree alone."

"Oh, I don't mind." And that was true. She was in a good mood; in fact, she planned to give Mrs. Mullinex the Sunday paper when she'd finished—and she'd leave the crossword untouched.

"Think of next year," Angie urged. "You'll most likely be married by then."

"John and me." She filled her head with happy thoughts of a Christmas photo in front of next year's tree, the two of them smiling blissfully into the camera. The perfect Christmas. The first card she mailed out would be to Jill and Tom.

"You might even be pregnant by then."

"Whoa, you're moving a little too fast."

"Why? You're getting the best husband money can buy, aren't you?"

Cassie laughed. She hadn't thought of it in those terms but Angie was right. She was paying top dollar to meet John-the-engineer; by the same token, he'd been willing to pay top dollar to meet her.

And the one walking away with fistfuls of cash was Simon Dodson.

As far as Cassie was concerned, he would have earned every penny.

Chapter 8

At the end of their brief telephone conversation, Angie had said she'd call Cassie once she got home Sunday evening. Although it'd been an offhand comment, Cassie was surprised when she didn't hear from her. Apparently Angie's last-minute meeting with her friend had turned into more of an event.

Cassie didn't think much about it until Angie showed up at the lab Monday morning. Her friend's face radiated...joy. Unmistakable joy.

"Well, well, well," Cassie said, watching Angie closely. Something was up, and it didn't take Sherlock Holmes to figure out that a man was involved. Clearly Angie had met someone special. The "old friend" from yesterday evening?

"Stop looking at me like that," Angie said, blushing.

"You're in love, aren't you?"

Angie's eyes widened. "You can tell? Really?"

Cassie nodded. "You've got the happy look. You know, the one we all get when we first realize we're falling for someone." She knew it had to be the "friend" Angie had seen last night.

Angie shyly glanced away. "The most incredible feeling came over me this morning." Her voice fell to a whisper. "It's like...a sixth sense, a knowledge, that this man could be the one."

"That's the feeling I'm talking about." Cassie had never experienced it herself, but she'd seen it again and again with her friends.

A wistful happiness shone from Angie's eyes, but she didn't say anything else.

After several minutes Cassie couldn't stand it anymore. "Well?" she asked.

The reflective look disappeared and was instantly replaced by one that was far more guarded. "Well, what?"

"Aren't you going to give me details?"

Angie hesitated. "Of course...but not yet."

This confused Cassie. First, there was very little they didn't tell each other—except for Angie's meeting with the matchmaker and it was easy to understand why her friend hadn't mentioned that, since Simon had rejected her as a client. If it'd happened to her, Cassie wouldn't have announced it, either. But this was an entirely different matter. For some reason, Angie preferred to remain tight-lipped about this man in her life. Well, so be it. When necessary, Cassie could be patient. If Angie wanted to keep this mystery man to herself for a while, Cassie would respect that.

"I'll tell you everything soon," Angie said. "It's just that I'd like to hold on to this feeling for a little longer."

Still, Cassie couldn't help being curious. "Would it hurt to let me know how you met?"

Angie's face relaxed into a warm smile. "You'll love that part. We sort of stumbled upon each other. We dated for a while ages ago and decided it wasn't going to work. Or rather, he did, not me. So I began the search again."

"So this is the guy you've been in love with all along?"

Angie nodded. "You'll meet him," she said a second time. "I promise."

"Will you be seeing him soon?"

"No. It's a bit...complicated at the moment."

"Complicated?" Cassie didn't like the sound of that. "He's not married or anything, is he?"

Angie shook her head. "Oh, no! Nothing like that."

"Good." Cassie smiled, then glanced down at her feet. "Actually," she said in a low voice, "I was hoping to chat with you last night. I had a couple of questions."

"What kind of questions?"

"I wanted to ask you about Simon."

"What about him?"

"Basically...I was curious. Other than the information on his Web site, what do you know?"

Angie shrugged. "Not much."

"How did you hear about him?"

"He was a birthday gift—at least, the first consultation was."

"Who from?"

"My mother. She wants grandchildren and knew how brokenhearted I was when...this other relationship ended. She heard about Simon when he did a radio interview."

"Simon did a radio interview?"

"I don't think he does them often. This was around Valentine's Day a few years back."

"Oh."

Angie cocked her head to one side. "Why this interest in Dr. Dodson all of a sudden?"

Cassie didn't want Angie or anyone to suspect how intrigued she was by the matchmaker. She found her thoughts drifting toward him far more often than was comfortable. She told herself that once her curiosity was satisfied, he'd drift into the background where he belonged.

While she'd gone on to his Web site—the address was noted on his business card—she hadn't searched further.

That evening, she did. She logged on to the Internet and immediately typed his name into Google. There wasn't a *lot,* but enough to answer some of her questions. He'd been a Rhodes scholar, attending Cambridge—after Harvard. He'd taught at a prestigious East Coast college. He'd written political articles for the *Wall Street Journal* and the *New York Times.* Just as she'd realized earlier, he had opinions about everything and didn't mind sharing them...in unvarnished prose.

According to Wikipedia, Simon had never been married. She found that…interesting.

Intent as she was on reading her computer screen, the phone startled her. "Yes," Cassie said, snatching it up. Her gaze stayed on the screen for fear she'd miss a single detail.

"Ms. Beaumont?" The female voice was vaguely familiar. "This is Dr. Dodson's office."

A chill raced down her spine. Simon knew she was online, reading about him! He was about to inform her that she'd forfeited her thirty thousand dollars. "I won't do it again!" she blurted without thinking.

"Excuse me?"

"Were you phoning because—" Cassie stopped abruptly, aware of how absurd she'd been. How paranoid. "Can I help you?" she asked sweetly.

By now Ms. Snelling sounded utterly confused. "Would it be convenient for you to stop by tomorrow afternoon at four-thirty?" she asked.

"Ah, sure." That meant leaving work a bit early, which wasn't really a problem.

"Thank you. Dr. Dodson will see you then."

Rattled as she was, Cassie had hung up before she

thought to ask what the meeting was about. She assumed Simon would be giving her the information regarding her second task. But why not call? Maybe he had her elf costume, although that seemed unlikely.

She felt a sense of expectation. She had to admit that Simon fascinated her, although she didn't especially like him—any more than he liked her. Perhaps he represented a challenge and she couldn't resist trying to make him aware of her as a woman. *Everyone* needed to be liked and appreciated, even Simon. That was probably what had led him into the matchmaking business. Certainly the couples she'd spoken to had expressed their appreciation—if not liking—for him. So maybe he couldn't achieve romantic satisfaction for himself but he could for others. It all seemed rather lonely.

On Tuesday, she kept checking her watch. Angie, who might otherwise have commented, was preoccupied, as well. Cassie had decided not to question her about this new, or rather resumed, relationship. When Angie was ready to tell her, she would. Cassie could only hope this man turned out to be everything Angie believed he was. Perhaps they could have a double wedding!

Because Simon had kept her waiting at their previous

appointments, Cassie didn't bother to show up until four forty-five. His assistant's disapproval was obvious. When Cassie stepped up to the desk, the older woman regarded her with distaste. "You're late."

"Well, yes... Simon, Dr. Dodson, was late the past two times and—"

"And you felt turnabout was fair play," he said, standing in the doorway leading to his office. "If you'll forgive the cliché." His arms were crossed and he looked more amused than annoyed.

It'd been four days since she'd last seen him and it struck her again how attractive he was.

He arched his brows. "You have nothing to say? Generally I can't get you to shut up and now you act as if we've never met."

"No...I figured you'd be late and—and I didn't want to waste time sitting here..." she stammered, embarrassed that he'd caught her staring.

"Don't let it happen again."

"Then don't keep me waiting again," she returned.

His shoulders relaxed. "Ah, I see the Cassie I recognize is back. Follow me. We have business to discuss." He walked into his office, Cassie close behind him.

Without waiting for an invitation, she took the visitor's chair across from his desk. She leaned back, legs crossed, trying to appear confident.

Looking stiff and formal once more, Simon sat down. "I asked to see you because I have the information concerning your agreement to work as Santa's helper."

She nodded. "Okay, but you could've phoned—unless you have my outfit."

"Outfit?"

"For my elf job."

Simon shook his head, and for the first time since she'd arrived, he seemed edgy. "There's been a small change in plans."

"Change? What do you mean?"

"The mall has experienced a decline in the number of parents bringing their children to meet Santa."

"Does this mean Santa won't be requiring my help, after all?" She did her best to keep her enthusiasm to a minimum. She wouldn't mind getting out of this; she liked children—in fact, she loved them—but if her tasks were limited to two instead of three, she'd be done that much sooner. Then Simon could introduce her to John.

Despite herself, she felt a twinge of regret at the idea

of never seeing Simon again. But once he'd made the official introduction, his role would be over, his job done. She realized she'd miss his acerbic responses....

Simon frowned at her. "What are you thinking?" he asked.

Cassie answered a bit more sharply than she'd intended. "I'm sure you're not interested in my thoughts."

Again his brows shot toward his hairline. "I wonder how long it will take you to learn that I do not ask questions unless I *am* interested in the answer."

Cassie threw back her head. "All right, fine. I was just thinking that you're a very odd man. I find I'm rather... intrigued by you. Not in any romantic way, of course."

"Of course," he said dryly. "I can't tell you what a relief that is."

"It's more like...driving past a car wreck. Horrible though it is, you can't stop yourself from looking."

His frown deepened. "I can assure you my life is no wreck—nor is my car."

"Yes, well, I'm sure there's nothing wrong with your car."

Ignoring her comment and its implication, Simon picked up a piece of paper. "As I was saying, I heard from the Tacoma Mall regarding your assignment. There's been a slight change."

"Is this because of what you said earlier—that there's a decline in the number of children visiting Santa?"

"Yes. But here's what—"

"Oh, wait, I have a question," Cassie broke in.

Simon looked up at the ceiling as though his patience, which was always in short supply, had been sorely tested yet again. "No."

"That's rather dictatorial," she said. "How could a question hurt?"

"If you'd let me get a word in edgewise… I'm trying to give you some important information."

"About helping Santa?" Simon acted as if she'd have to smuggle top secret papers to the north pole.

"This relates directly to your assignment," he said, avoiding eye contact. "I need to know if you're afraid of heights."

How could that possibly pertain to her working as an elf? "Not really. Why?"

Simon paused. "Maybe you should ask me your question, after all, before I explain."

"I'd rather hear what you have to say first."

He sighed loudly. "I talked to the mall and—"

"Yes, yes, we've been through this."

"I did mention that a uniform—a costume—is required."

"Yes." His reluctance to get to the point was beginning to concern her.

"I wasn't aware anything like this would be asked of you, but I'm encouraged that you don't have any fear of heights."

"I don't have to swing from the top of the Space Needle, do I?"

"No..." He exhaled slowly, staring down at his desk. "The mall wants the first elf—that would be you—to arrive by wire."

Cassie swallowed hard. "You're not referring to a telegram, are you?"

"No."

"A wire...from where?"

Again he avoided meeting her gaze. "The ceiling."

Cassie frowned, attempting to picture it. "You mean they want me to fly in like Peter Pan?"

"Exactly."

"You're joking!" This was the most preposterous idea she'd ever heard.

"The reindeer will follow you."

"*Live* reindeer?"

"They're plastic, but the mall wants to make a real production of Santa's arrival."

"And," she said, swallowing again since her mouth was so dry, "I'm part of the production."

"Yes. Are you willing to do this?" he asked.

Cassie's fingers tightened around her purse strap. "Would I still meet John if I decline?"

Simon hesitated. "This wasn't part of our original agreement, so I'd need to find a replacement task. That might take a few weeks."

"I don't want to wait any longer than I already have to."

"Then I'll inform the mall there won't be a problem and they can expect you on Saturday morning around nine."

Her complete lack of reaction must have alerted Simon to the fact that she was having second thoughts.

"No need to worry," Simon assured her. "I've been told it's quite safe. The wire will hold up to four hundred pounds."

"Oh." Cassie couldn't believe she'd agreed to this. When she glanced up, she thought, just for a moment, that she saw a smile on Simon's face. She leaned forward. "Were you smiling?"

"Pardon me?"

"You were smiling, weren't you? You're enjoying this." The man should be arrested for deriving pleasure from her humiliation.

His mouth quivered, but Simon had the good grace to look away. "Actually, I was thinking you're going to manage this quite well. You're a woman who's destined for high places."

Unfortunately, his vote of confidence didn't excite her. And his joke didn't amuse her.

Chapter 9

Simon says: The best match for you is the one I arrange—because I know you better than you know yourself.

"This must be a joke," Cassie said, staring at the limp green tights. No way was she going to stuff her hips and thighs into those.

"Dr. Dodson gave us your size, miss," said an elderly woman, whose name tag identified her as Daisy.

"He did?" Well, if he assumed she wore a size four, then who was she to enlighten him with the truth? Besides, the material did stretch.

Daisy handed her the elf costume, which consisted of a short green dress, like a skater's, with white faux fur edging the hem and a wide red belt. A green Santa-style hat with a white fur ball dangling from the end completed the outfit. But the pièce de résistance was a gold-painted pair of slippers with curled-up toes.

"The changing room is this way," Daisy said as she guided her down the dimly lit mall corridor.

Cassie followed, clutching the uniform, the hat and shoes.

"I can't tell you how pleased we are that you agreed to do this," Daisy was telling her. "You already have an audience of children waiting."

This wasn't news Cassie wanted to hear. "Where will Santa be while I'm floating through the air?"

"Oh, he'll be right behind you."

"Great." So she wouldn't be doing a solo flight. If she was going to descend from the clouds, Santa should do the same.

"Only...Santa will be on ground level," Daisy explained.

This was unfair.

The woman stopped and, frowning, bent down to pick up an empty beer can. "Oh, dear," she grumbled. "I'm afraid Floyd's been at it again."

"And who is Floyd?" Cassie asked a bit fearfully.

Daisy's voice was a low whisper. "He's Santa."

Was she saying Santa was a *drunk?* Outrageous!

"Santa?" Cassie cried.

"Don't misunderstand me," Daisy hurried to say. "Floyd's a wonderful Santa and the kids love him. The problem is, the children can be a bit wearing...as you'll discover for yourself in a few minutes." Daisy led her through a dark tunnel to some kind of alleyway deep inside the mall. "There's a ladies' room back here where you can change into your costume. I'll wait outside and once you're done, I'll have one of the technicians help you into the harness."

Cassie gaped at her.

"We want you to be as safe as possible," Daisy said in a confiding voice. "The wire will lower you from the top level of the mall to the ground floor."

"Oh." Cassie couldn't recall if the mall was two or three levels. One thing was guaranteed—she'd have her eyes closed the entire flight.

As if reading her mind, Daisy added, "You have to play this up, you know."

"Play this up?" Cassie asked skeptically. "What do you mean?"

"To the crowd. We want you to yell out that Santa's on his way and all the boys and girls will be getting a gift from him."

"We're giving them gifts?"

"Candy canes. The children look forward to receiving those."

A cheap candy cane was a gift? That seemed to be an exaggeration—but who was Cassie to quibble over truth in advertising?

They finally got to the ladies' room and Cassie went inside. She removed her shoes and then her jeans and sweater. She hung what she could on the hook of the stall door, then sat on the toilet in order to slip on the tights. *Force* them on was more accurate.

The fit was so tight, they felt like an extra skin. Unfortunately they didn't reach all the way to her waist. One wrong move, and Cassie feared they'd roll down and reveal features—like her butt—that she'd rather keep private. It helped a little to jump up and down and then prance around, pulling on the waistband as she did. She also did a couple of squats. Still, the tights didn't stretch quite as far as she would've liked.

"Is everything all right in there, dear?" Daisy asked.

"Just fine," Cassie told her. Thankfully, the minidress fit. The shoes were good, too. She adjusted the hat in the bathroom mirror and realized she'd need to secure it for the flight. Digging around the bottom of her purse, she located two paper clips, which worked—sort of. How long those paper clips had been there and where they'd come from would forever remain a mystery. Cassie could only be grateful for their presence.

She opened the restroom door, feeling more than a little foolish.

Daisy stood back and brought both hands to her face. "Oh, this is just perfect."

"I look okay?"

"You look *wonderful*. The children are going to be so excited." Daisy glanced at her watch, then led Cassie to an elevator. Silently they rode to the second floor, where a crew of men seemed to be waiting for her. Eight—or was it nine?—life-size plastic reindeer were lined up against the wall beside an authentic-looking sleigh.

Before Cassie had a chance to ask any questions, two of the men stepped forward and strapped her into a harness. They moved her arms, each grasping one, lifting them up and down.

One of the men murmured something in Spanish. She couldn't understand what he'd said, but got the gist of it when he made the sign of the cross and raised his eyes heavenward.

"Don't look down," the other man advised her tersely.

"You don't have a thing to worry about," Daisy said with a grandmotherly smile.

Suddenly a voice came over the loudspeaker system. "Boys and girls, moms and dads—is that Santa's sleigh I hear?"

The man next to her jingled bells and everyone looked up to where Cassie stood.

"Okay, boys," Daisy whispered and stepped back.

Suddenly Cassie was hoisted from the ground. Her feet made running movements as she scrabbled to find her footing and instead found only air.

"Play to the crowd," Daisy instructed in a loud stage whisper.

"Santa's on his way!" Cassie called out, doing her best to sound enthusiastic although she was absolutely terrified. "I can see him now! Look, here comes Santa."

And then it happened. Cassie gasped as her tights rolled down, catching on her thighs. She didn't know what to do. The tights slid farther down and everyone in the entire mall seemed to be staring up at her.

"I can see the elf's underpants," a little boy called, pointing at her.

Suspended above the ground, Cassie watched as several mothers covered their children's eyes.

"Get her to the ground fast," Cassie heard Daisy hiss.

The men released the rope and Cassie plunged downward. "Yiiiiiii!" she screamed, all the while struggling to pull up her tights. She'd partially succeeded—then saw that she was about to make a crash landing.

Just when it seemed she was destined to slam into the ground, a tall man emerged from the crowd and deftly caught her in his arms. The impact would have been enough to send them both sprawling to the floor if not for the fact that he'd braced his feet. Together they staggered backward until her hero recovered his balance.

Cassie opened her eyes to see that the stranger who'd rescued her wasn't a stranger at all. Her startled eyes met Simon's, and they both breathed a sigh of relief. For a long moment, they stared at each other. Cassie's arms were tightly wrapped around his neck. It took time for her to find her voice and, when she did, it came out in a high-pitched squeal.

"You're paying for this," she told him, her pulse hammering in her ears. Why she'd ever agreed to this ridiculous scenario she'd never know. One thing was for sure; there wouldn't be a repeat performance.

Simon lowered her to the ground. "A simple thank-you will suffice," he said calmly.

Fortunately the audience was distracted by the flying reindeer, and no one could hear her X-rated response. Santa made his appearance, slipping out from behind a curtain. Santa Floyd carried a large bag over his shoulder, presumably filled with candy canes.

Santa ascended to his special chair, a huge cushioned monstrosity set up on the curtained dais, and Cassie took her place beside him. She looked around for Simon but he was nowhere in sight. The boys and girls lined up with their parents, and the photographer was ready with his camera.

The first boy clung to his mother. "He's a little scared," the woman explained, prying her son loose from her leg.

The poor kid was panic-stricken. Cassie couldn't understand why the mother felt it was so important to make him sit on Santa's lap.

"There's no need to be frightened." Cassie crouched down and tried to reassure the boy, who couldn't have been more than four years old.

"Go away!" he shouted.

Cassie straightened and stepped back. Her timing was perfect. The boy, without even a hint of warning, vomited on one of her shoes.

"Oh, dear. I'm so sorry," the mother said a dozen times. "I had no idea Jason was going to do that."

Cassie hopped around on one foot until the photographer produced a small towel. If Jason was any indication of what she should expect, Cassie could only imagine the rest of her day.

"Why don't you sit on Santa's lap with your son," the photographer suggested. The mother appeared eager to do anything that would remove attention from Cassie and the results of her son's queasy stomach. She clambered onto Floyd's lap, her son dangling from her arms.

After cleaning off her shoe, Cassie returned to her duties. The next few children had obviously had prior experience. They all told Santa their Christmas wishes, rattling off everything on their lists.

The line moved relatively well for the next half hour

or so. There was the occasional crying baby and one pair of twins who took up more time than allotted, but all in all, it was a smooth-running operation.

Cassie had worked about two hours of her three-hour shift and was just beginning to think this job was tolerable. A lot of the children, while frightened, were eager to meet Santa. "Who are *you?*" a little girl asked as she waited patiently for her turn some time later. Cassie's shift was almost over by then, and there were only a few more kids in line. Other than a harrowing entrance and one small boy with a queasy stomach, it hadn't worked out so badly.

"Who am I?" Cassie repeated the question. "I'm one of Santa's helpers," she said as she handed the child a candy cane.

"Are you really an elf?"

Cassie nodded.

"You don't look like an elf."

"I don't?" Cassie said, surprised.

"You look more like a—"

"You pushed in front of me," the child's mother protested, elbowing the woman ahead of her in line.

"I most certainly did not!" The second woman elbowed the other one back as her son watched, eyes wide.

"Mommy, I have to pee." This plaintive declaration came from the first combatant's daughter, aged four or five.

"We are not getting out of this line now. I'll find you a restroom as soon as we're done," she said and shoved her way to the front, dragging the little girl.

"Would you kindly tell this person that I was ahead of her?" The comment was directed at Cassie by the other woman. The shoving match continued.

"Sorry," Cassie said, coming to stand between the two mothers. "I really wasn't paying attention, but if this goes on, I'm afraid I'll have to ask you both to leave." She said this with great authority and was rather proud of herself.

"Mommy," the little girl cried, her voice urgent now. "I can't wait anymore."

That was when Cassie felt the warm liquid soak into the top of her foot. She glanced down and saw a small waterfall raining down, ruining her undamaged shoe—the one unstained by vomit.

Letting out a yell, she leaped back and automatically shook her foot.

"Orange!" the woman shouted.

"It's okay. I don't have to pee anymore."

"Oh, dear…"

"Your daughter's name is Orange?" the other woman asked.

The first woman nodded. "We're from Florida."

The second mother backed away from the puddle on the floor, clutching her son's hand—and leaving Orange at the head of the line.

"I have a tissue." Orange's mother—Grapefruit? Cassie thought hysterically—offered her a crumpled wad.

"I'm fine," Cassie muttered. She intended to burn these tights once her shift was over. The shoes were probably goners, too. She wondered if Simon could possibly have known what this stint would entail.

After the two squabbling mothers had finished with Santa, a young girl, the very last one in line, approached Cassie all by herself.

"She hasn't paid," the photographer said as he returned his camera to its case.

Pleading eyes were raised to Cassie's. "I need to talk to Santa for just a minute," the girl whispered. "You don't have to give me a candy cane."

"How old are you?" Cassie asked, bending down so they were eye-to-eye.

"Eight."

Just a bit too old to believe in Santa Claus. And yet the child was so intent, Cassie didn't feel she could turn her away.

"Forget about the picture," she said when the photographer cast her a dirty look.

"Ho. Ho. Ho. And who do we have here?" Santa asked, ignoring the other man. He held out his arms to the child.

"Catherine," the child said softly. She walked up to Santa but didn't sit on his lap.

"And what would you like for Christmas?" he asked, playing his role to the hilt.

Staring down at the carpet, the child said, "I want my daddy to come home." Huge tears welled in her eyes. "He left and now my mommy says they're getting a divorce. All I want for Christmas is my daddy back."

Cassie felt tears burning in her own eyes. She looked at Floyd and wondered how he'd handle this.

"That's a mighty big order, Catherine," he said.

"I don't want anything else. I don't need toys but I need my daddy."

"Catherine?" A woman's voice echoed through the mall.

"I'm here, Mommy!"

The child's mother rushed up the steps to Santa's throne and fell to her knees in front of her daughter. She seemed about to burst into tears. "I looked *everywhere* for you," she cried. She threw her arms around her daughter's waist.

"I told you I was going to talk to Santa," Catherine reminded her. "I had to wait in line."

"I'm sorry if Catherine caused a problem," her mother said and, standing, took the little girl by the hand—but not before Santa whispered a few words in the child's ear.

"We're finished," Santa said as Catherine's mother led her daughter away.

Cassie must have looked as upset as she felt because Floyd gently patted her back. "Those are the tough ones. You did a great job."

Cassie doubted that.

"What did you say to her?" she asked him.

"I said her daddy still loves her and that he'll always love her. That it's not her fault he left." He stretched his arms high above his head. "Now this Santa has an appointment with Mr. Budweiser. Want to join me?"

"Thanks...but no thanks."

"Then you're free to go. Another elf will take over for you this afternoon."

Cassie nodded, eager to make her escape. As she started for the changing room, Simon appeared beside her.

Cassie realized she wasn't going to be able to control her emotions. Tears streamed down her face.

"What is it?" he asked. He seemed genuinely concerned.

"I was that little girl once," she said with difficulty. "All I wanted for Christmas was for my daddy to come home." She covered her mouth with both hands, trying to stifle her sobs.

They reached the doorway that led to the mall interior. Simon held open the door and Cassie slipped into the darkened hallway. Once inside, she leaned against the wall and let the tears flow unrestrained.

Simon stood next to her for several minutes, then tentatively placed his arms around her.

Cassie didn't care who he was; she needed his comfort. She rested her face against him, sobbing into his expensive wool jacket.

His hold relaxed and, after an awkward moment, he spoke soothingly into her ear. She couldn't make out what he was saying. It didn't matter.

As if by instinct, she lifted her head and gazed up at him. He whispered something else, something that sounded like "It wasn't your fault." Then his lips, warm and tender, descended on hers.

Chapter 10

Simon says: If you're the woman he's looking for, I will find you.

Simon's gentleness consoled her as he held her close. Cassie didn't want him to ever stop, and he didn't seem inclined to let her go. Time lost meaning, and Cassie didn't know how long he held her against him.

Then, just when she was least prepared, he seemed to snap to attention, become aware of his surroundings. He dropped his arms and stepped away. His movements were so abrupt that she nearly stumbled. She might have if he hadn't clasped her shoulders to steady her.

Speechless, she stared up at him, unable to make sense of what had happened in the past few minutes. Under normal conditions, Cassie didn't give way to emotion, and certainly not in public. But Christmas, that little girl and the memory of losing her own father had struck her hard and there'd been no stopping the barrage of deeply buried feelings. She told herself she was *not* going to react to that kiss.

"I need a cup of coffee," she murmured. Despite her tears her throat was parched.

Simon nodded.

"I'll change clothes and be right back." She was sure her voice sounded strained and unnatural. She hurried inside the ladies' room; once the door was closed she leaned against it and covered her face. Her whole body was trembling. Eventually, when she felt composed again, she straightened and began to dress.

To the best of her knowledge, this was the first time she'd ever cried over her father. Peter Beaumont had simply walked out of their lives one day as if it meant nothing. As if *they* meant nothing. The event had forever marked her and Shawn and their mother, as well. And yet he seemed oblivious to the anguish he'd inflicted on his wife and children. His excuse was that he needed to "find himself." Apparently he couldn't manage that and be a husband and father at the same time. His was a solitary path, and it didn't seem to matter how many hearts he crushed along the way. Cassie made every effort to cast all thoughts of him out of her mind. But he was there, as much as she wanted to deny his existence.

When Cassie had finished dressing, she left her outfit neatly on a ledge near the sink and wrote Daisy a note explaining why the shoes and tights were in the garbage. Then she brushed her hair and repaired her makeup. Simon was pacing in the hallway outside the door. He stopped when he saw her and even in the dimly lit hallway she could see that he wasn't quite himself, either.

With his hand at her elbow, he escorted her back into the mall and toward an exit. "There's a place close by where we can have coffee." He reached inside his pocket for his car keys. "I'll drive."

Cassie didn't know what was wrong with the restaurants that were within walking distance. However, she didn't have the energy to argue, so she just followed him.

She wasn't surprised to see that he drove a black sedan with a black interior, which was meticulously maintained; she wouldn't have expected anything less. Simon wasn't the type of man who'd have hamburger wrappings and stale French fries littering his vehicle.

They didn't speak; he glanced at her for approval, then flipped on a CD. She recognized the calming strains of a Bach piano concerto. Again, she wasn't surprised, although she couldn't have identified the piece. She leaned back, eyes shut, letting the music flow over her. The restaurant wasn't really all that close, she noted a little later. It was perhaps a fifteen-minute drive along the Tacoma waterfront before he pulled into an exclusive housing development. He turned down several streets, then entered a driveway.

"This isn't a restaurant," Cassie said.

"No, it's my home."

"Your home?"

"I felt we'd both appreciate privacy for this discussion."

He was probably right.

Simon ushered her inside. The house was spotless. It looked like one of those model homes with everything carefully arranged and color-coordinated, not a thing out of place. No Christmas decorations. Nor did she see a single photograph, and that seemed almost unnatural. Surely there were people in his life, people he loved and cared about. Family. Friends. Then again, maybe he preferred to keep his distance from others. Maybe he felt his job required it.

"Make yourself comfortable," he said and gestured toward the sofa. Then he disappeared into the kitchen through a swinging door.

Cassie looked out over Commencement Bay, although her thoughts still churned and she hardly noticed the beauty before her. She had a distinct feeling that their professional agreement was about to come to an end.

Other than one brief interchange—when he asked how she liked her coffee—all was silent.

After a few minutes, Simon reappeared with two cups of coffee. He handed her one, careful to avoid physical contact, before taking a seat as far away as the room allowed. He stared down at his coffee. "I would like to know what happened back at the mall," he said after a tense moment.

"Okay." It wasn't as if they could ignore the episode. "Which part do you want to discuss?"

"What were those tears about?"

Now Cassie stared into her coffee. "My father," she began, then shook her head. "The last child in line."

"The little girl who was by herself?"

"Yes. She came to Santa because..." The lump in her throat made it necessary to pause and swallow before she could continue. "She didn't want toys or clothes or gifts, she...she wanted her daddy back."

"Ah." Simon's eyes softened with understanding and what looked like sympathy. "She reminded you of yourself at that age. You said as much, didn't you?"

Cassie nodded. "My father left during the holidays. So he not only broke our hearts, he made sure Christmas would never be the same."

"He sounds like a real jewel of a human being," Simon said disdainfully.

But Cassie didn't wish her father ill. He'd paid for his mistakes; in his late sixties now, he was essentially alone. While she liked to think she'd put all the bitterness behind her, she didn't really have a relationship with him, nor did she seek one. Every so often, Pete made the effort to contact her, but they had nothing in common, nothing to talk about, nothing to share. The conversation typically lasted a few minutes. Invariably Cassie felt sad afterward.

"I don't want you to assume I'm the kind of woman who breaks into tears at the drop of a hat. I... It was like seeing myself all those years ago. Like feeling pain so raw it tore my heart out." Her voice quavered and she tried to conceal it by sipping coffee.

"Pain and the memory of pain—which often amounts to the same thing—don't really go away," Simon said. "That's why we have to learn to assimilate it."

She nodded.

Simon didn't say anything else for some time. "I believe it would be best if we..."

He stopped speaking, which made Cassie look at him.

"That kiss," he murmured, shifting his weight.

Seeing Simon ill at ease was so unusual she couldn't help enjoying it, although that was probably unkind of her. At least it was a distraction from her own painful past. "Yes, the kiss."

He frowned. "I want to assure you I don't make a habit of kissing my clients."

She instinctively recognized that as the truth.

"Weeping women don't generally affect me like that, either. I don't have any excuse and I wish to apologize."

His gaze held hers and she couldn't doubt the sincerity of his words. "I was as much at fault as you," she felt obliged to admit. "I—"

"I will refund your money," he said, cutting her off.

It was what she'd been afraid of. "But why?"

"I stepped over the line. This is the only way I can rectify the...incident."

Cassie bit her lip. She conceded that the kiss shouldn't have happened. But that wasn't a good reason to ruin everything. "Will I still meet John?" she asked, then held her breath, almost afraid of what he'd say. She was practically gasping for air by the time he replied.

"Considering that I was the one who initiated the... incident, I feel honor-bound to hold up my part of the bargain."

"If that's the case, then that kiss just cost you thirty thousand dollars."

He didn't look any too pleased with himself, but merely shrugged. "So be it. This was a lesson well learned."

"I don't feel I can let you do that." Tempting as it was for Cassie to accept, fair was fair. She hadn't exactly pushed him away. In fact, she'd welcomed his kiss, welcomed his comfort.

"I am not in the habit of arguing with my clients."

"Or with anyone, it seems."

He blinked as if it took him a moment to comprehend what she'd said. "Or with anyone," he agreed.

She sighed. "I appreciate the offer, Simon, really I do, but you weren't the only one who learned a lesson. How about if we both forget it ever happened and just move forward?"

"Fine," he said curtly. "I would like your promise that you'll never mention our kiss again. Can you do that?"

She nodded. "Yes. Of course."

"Good. I'll undertake to do the same thing."

She mimed zipping her lips closed. "It's gone, forgotten, cast into the deepest part of the ocean." The thought flashed into her mind that the ocean was filled with treasures—treasures no one even knew were there. When it happened, Simon's kiss had felt like treasure, unexpected and...beautiful.

"My plan for the third task is to have you cook Christmas dinner," he reminded her.

Cassie raised her hand. "Yes, I wanted to talk to you about that."

"What about it?"

She might as well be blunt. "Like I told you before, I don't have the best neighbors."

"What precisely is the problem?"

Cassie sat up straighter. The Simon she recognized was back. He wasn't interested in listening to any excuses—except that in this instance excuses were necessary. Cassie couldn't possibly invite her neighbors to Christmas dinner. She didn't really know these people, and what she did know unnerved her.

"Out with it, Cassie. I don't have all day."

Hiding her smile would have been impossible.

"What's that silly grin for?" he demanded in the gruff voice she'd grown accustomed to.

"You. You're back!"

"I never left."

"But you did," she said. "A few minutes ago, while we were discussing—you know, what we promised never to mention again—you seemed...almost human."

His left brow rose, mocking her. "*Almost,* you say?"

"Yes—and I rather liked it."

"Don't get used to it."

"Oh, not to worry. I won't." She set her coffee aside and sat on her hands. "Anyway, continue."

"We were discussing your third task."

"I feel you should know that one of my neighbors, Mrs. Mullinex, is a thief."

"She has a police record?"

"I... No, I don't think so. But who knows? Anyone who'd purposely take my newspaper..."

"Your *newspaper?*"

"Yes, that's what she's been stealing for the last few months." Then, stricken by an attack of conscience, Cassie went on to explain. "To be honest, Mrs. Mullinex does return it, but she clips out the coupons. Then, a couple of weeks back, she went so far as to take the Sunday edition, and get this—she likes to do the Sunday *New York Times* crossword puzzle. *My* crossword puzzle." She narrowed her eyes. "I wouldn't have to invite her, would I?"

"Oh, yes."

"And Mr. Oliver?"

"What's wrong with Mr. Oliver?"

Cassie had no qualms about detailing her other neighbor's faults. "First, he's rude. More than once, Mr. Oliver has deliberately allowed the elevator doors to close on me." She wagged her index finger at Simon. "I'm positive he could see me, too. I saw that gleam in his eyes. The Sunday before last he left me standing there, loaded down with groceries, and he *enjoyed* it."

"I...see." Once more he seemed unimpressed by her tales of woe.

"Then there's the guy whose condo's next to mine. I don't know his name and I don't want to. He plays his music so loud it shakes my whole kitchen. It's horrible music, too. Rap and heavy metal." She paused. "Now here's the interesting part."

"I can hardly wait."

Simon might be making fun of her, but Cassie forged on. "I saw him in the hallway for the first time this week. All along I'd assumed that whoever he was, he must be college age. This guy was *old.* He had to be sixty if he was a day."

Having laid out her case, Cassie felt certain that Simon would understand why she wouldn't want to go to all that effort for these people. "So you'll reconsider?" she asked him.

"Reconsider what?"

"Giving me a different third task. Surely even you can see it would be impossible to put on a festive dinner for my neighbors."

"No, after hearing this, I believe the third task will be perfect."

Chapter 11

Simon says: The perfect neighbor is the one who's never home.

"You mean you *won't* reconsider?" Cassie sputtered. Simon was being totally unreasonable.

"Did you or did you not agree to host this dinner?"

"Well, yes," she admitted with some reluctance, "but that was before I realized I'd be obliged to fly through the air with my underwear showing." A little guilt on his part might not be amiss.

"A small wardrobe malfunction."

He said it with a straight face and Cassie stared at him, wondering if this was meant to be a joke. "I suppose you could call it that."

"At least you didn't have a television audience."

She rolled her eyes. "Yeah, that makes it better."

"Regardless, you are still required to complete a third task."

Cassie made a face. "You're a cruel man, Dr. Dodson."

"You were well aware of the conditions of our agreement before you signed the contract. However..."

"Yes?" Hope filled her.

"However, I believe it might be advantageous if you served this dinner *prior* to Christmas. In other words, not on Christmas Day itself as I originally specified."

"Advantageous how?"

"If you agree to this new stipulation, I'll arrange for you to meet John before the twenty-fifth."

"Oh." Cassie had her suspicions. "And when did you make this decision?" She wasn't fooled; Simon wanted her gone and on her way to marital bliss so he wouldn't have to deal with her anymore.

"Why the dirty look? I would think you'd be grateful."

"I'd be a whole lot more grateful if I didn't distrust your motives."

Simon watched her steadily. "And what is wrong with my motives?"

Irritated, Cassie stood. She wasn't sure why his latest suggestion upset her—the opposite *should* be true. It should thrill her, since she'd be that much closer to meeting John. But it didn't. She walked over to the picture window. "You want me out of your life," she mumbled, her back to him.

"I didn't say that."

"You didn't need to."

"Listen, Cassie, and this is important. Don't fall in love with me. I'm not good husband material. Furthermore—"

"Oh, please," she snapped. "You're in greater danger of falling for me!"

"Don't flatter yourself." He went into the kitchen with their coffee cups. When he came back, she guessed it was time to leave. Her clue was that he'd put on his coat and scarf.

On the return trip to the mall, there was silence between them, no music, not even the radio. When they arrived, Cassie told him where to drop her off. Simon pulled up behind her parked car.

"Please let me know when you intend to serve the Christmas meal," he said.

"Can I get back to you?"

He kept his hands on the steering wheel and gazed straight ahead. "Fine. But remember that all three tasks must be completed to my satisfaction. So far, you've done well."

Was that praise? From the high and mighty Simon Dodson? She could hardly believe it. He *must* have an ulterior motive, no matter how much he claimed otherwise. Although, now that she considered it, he hadn't exactly denied her accusation. "I'll call you later in the week with the date."

"Good. I thought you'd come around."

She opened the passenger door, then climbed out and banged it shut. *"Good,"* she mimicked. Seeing someone waiting eagerly for her parking space, Cassie hurriedly got into her car and backed out.

On the drive home she did her best to analyze why someone she disliked could affect her so profoundly. It troubled her that she'd enjoyed Simon's touch and his kiss, that she felt invigorated by his—occasionally annoying—conversation.

Not until the following Wednesday was Cassie able to work out a date that was agreeable to all her neighbors, as well as Angie and Shawn. Dinner was scheduled for the Sunday before Christmas.

To her credit, Mrs. Mullinex seemed pleased by the invitation and offered to bring her special pickled brussels sprouts. Her mother's recipe, she said. Cassie declined, saying she'd take care of everything.

Mr. Oliver gave a one-word answer. "Why?"

"It's just an invitation to dinner," Cassie said. "I'm doing all the cooking and...and it seemed neighborly to have a Christmas celebration." The explanation struck her as a bit lame, but she could hardly tell him her *real* reason.

"Who else are you inviting?"

She told him.

"I suppose I could come," he said and closed the door. He made it sound as if he was doing her a favor. In retrospect, maybe he was.

The rap-music man was harder to catch. She rang his doorbell several times, then pounded hard, but either he didn't want to answer or he was so deaf he couldn't hear her. In the end she slipped a note under his door.

He responded in kind, placing a message under her door that said he'd be delighted to join her for dinner. He signed it *Bob,* which seemed a rather inoffensive name for someone who listened to such belligerent music.

Now that the arrangements were made, Cassie was ready to contact Simon. She knew he kept evening hours a couple of days a week for the benefit of working clients, and this was one of those days.

"He's not in the office," Ms. Snelling informed her. "I don't see your name on the appointment list."

"He asked me to call." Or maybe she'd volunteered; Cassie couldn't remember.

"I see. Do you wish to leave a message for him?"

"No." Cassie was emphatic about that. She preferred to speak to him personally. In her opinion, it was time that he learned the art of compromise. She was going to ask for one small concession, and if Simon had any common sense at all, he'd agree.

"Can you tell me when he'll be available?"

"Oh, dear, I'm afraid I can't. Dr. Dodson is home sick with the flu."

Simon was sick? Cassie felt immediate sympathy. "How long has he been out?"

"Two days, and when he phoned in, he sounded absolutely dreadful."

"Poor man." Cassie hung up and went about her business. Her apartment looked Christmassy, thanks primarily to her brother's tree. She'd draped it with merrily twinkling lights that brought a festive quality to the dark evening. Cassie had added a trio of angels to the fireplace mantel. A lovely wreath hung on the inside, rather than the outside, of her door because she didn't trust her neighbors (one in particular) not to steal it.

Even with Christmas music playing in the background and cookbooks strewn across the kitchen counter, all Cassie could think about was Simon, sick and in bed. He was alone. He'd never mentioned family. She didn't know about friends, either. As far as she could tell, there was no one to check up on him. If she'd had a special recipe for chicken noodle soup she would've made him a pot of it.

Then it came to her—why *not* make him some soup? Medicinal soup for a friend. Simon might not consider her a friend, but Cassie couldn't ignore the fact that he might need someone. She began paging through her cookbooks. . . .

She didn't fool herself into believing Simon would appreciate the effort. But even knowing he'd probably resent her dropping off the soup wasn't enough to change her mind.

"You're going to a lot of trouble for him," Angie told her the next morning at work, when Cassie brought in a full quart of her concoction.

"That's true," she said, finding space in the lunchroom fridge for her plastic container.

"Why would you care? He's such a difficult man. I bet he'll bite your head off for making him get out of bed to answer the door."

Cassie nodded.

"How do you know where he lives, anyway?"

Rather than launch into the whole complicated tale, she said, "It's a long story. I'll save it for when we have more time."

"I'm holding you to that."

Fortunately, two colleagues joined them for lunch, so Cassie was spared the necessity of telling Angie what had happened on Saturday, when she'd been an elf. After work she called Simon's office and learned he was still sick. Her decision made, Cassie drove to Tacoma. She had no problem locating the neighborhood but had to drive around numerous streets before she found his house.

By then, it was completely dark and the rain fell in sheets. Racing from the car to his front door, carrying her quart container, she shook the moisture out of her hair before she rang his doorbell. When no one answered, she was tempted to leave the soup on his porch and drive away.

Just as she turned to do exactly that, the door opened and Simon stood there in his housecoat and slippers. He looked even worse than she might have imagined, with a pale face, rumpled hair and rheumy eyes. Her sympathy was instantly aroused and it was all she could do not to reach out and test his brow for fever.

"Cassie?"

She hadn't planned what she'd say, and now her tongue seemed to twist itself into knots. "I heard you were sick.... I—I brought you some homemade chicken noodle soup."

He stared at her as if he wasn't sure whether he was hallucinating.

"How are you feeling?" she asked, although the answer was obvious.

"Terrible." He stepped aside, silently inviting her into the house.

Cassie hadn't expected that. In fact, she'd been sure that he'd be angry. She'd expected him to growl and demand that she leave.

"I can't stay long. Like I said, I wanted to drop off the soup and tell you the turkey dinner's set for Sunday."

Simon covered his mouth and coughed. It resembled a dog's barking and seemed to rack his entire body. She wondered if he had pneumonia.

"Have you seen a doctor?" she asked urgently.

"I'll be fine. Don't fuss, Cassie."

"Someone should. Now, lie down and I'll heat up this soup." Taking charge, she walked past him and into his kitchen, which to her shock was untidy. Dishes littered the counter and pots were stacked in the sink. She could see that he'd made an effort to straighten up but had either grown too tired or was too sick to continue.

Before she started heating the soup, she placed the dirty dishes in the dishwasher and turned it on. Her soup warmed on the stove as she cleaned up the kitchen. Simon had disappeared and now returned dressed in slacks and a sweater. He'd apparently showered, because his hair was wet and combed.

"This is thoughtful of you." He actually sounded grateful.

Dishcloth in hand, Cassie regarded him suspiciously. "You mean to say you're not angry?"

"Why would I be angry?"

"I'm invading your privacy."

He acknowledged that with a slight tilt of his head.

The soup began to boil and Cassie removed the pan from the burner, poured some in a bowl and set it on the kitchen table with a spoon.

While Simon had his soup, she made them both cups of strong, hot tea, then sat across from him at the table. She declined his suggestion of soup, since she was too nervous to eat.

"This might surprise you, but I quite like you when you're sick."

He set the spoon next to his bowl and studied her warily. "I beg your pardon?"

That must have sounded strange. "You're more human when you're vulnerable." He didn't respond.

Cassie was gratified to see that he finished the entire bowlful of soup.

"Shall we have our tea in the living room?" she asked, noting that the television was on, the volume low.

Simon nodded. "I've watched more television in the past three days than the previous three years."

"Oh, *Jeopardy!*'s just starting. That's my favorite game show," she said, sitting on the couch. Simon sat beside her, a careful distance away—not too close and not too far.

He picked up the remote and turned up the volume. The thirty minutes passed quickly. She couldn't resist shouting out answers—"What is the Battle of Gettysburg?" "Who are Sacco and Vanzetti?" "What is silver nitrate?" She was pleased that she was almost always right, although she noticed that Simon didn't participate at all. He must be feeling very ill.

"I should leave," she said after Final Jeopardy ("Who was St. Nicholas?") and started to stand.

Simon reached for her hand. "Stay a while longer, if you don't mind."

"I don't..." The sudden surge of tenderness she felt

shocked her. What shocked her even more was that his hand continued to hold hers. His touch was light, but sometime during the next thirty minutes he intertwined their fingers. It was hard to concentrate on the rerun of *Frasier*—a Christmas episode she'd already seen—when her whole body was focused on his hand holding hers. Innocent enough on the surface, his action was highly sensual in its effect. She felt his touch in every part of her, in every sensitized nerve, every cell. She needed all her self-control not to turn into his arms and beg him to kiss her.

"My brother might be at the dinner," she said, hoping she didn't sound as breathless as she felt.

"I'd enjoy meeting him."

"You would? Angie might be able to come, too."

"Angie?"

"My best friend. You met her—and rejected her."

"Ah, yes, I remember her now."

"I wish you'd given her a chance," Cassie murmured.

"I couldn't. She was in love with someone and refused to admit it."

"How do you know?" she asked.

"It's my job. That's the point of such a detailed questionnaire. I explore people's responses and I read between the lines." He looked at her sternly, their hands still linked. "You know I can't discuss this with you."

"Oh." Her mouth had gone dry. If Simon could read others so well, she wondered if he was aware of the intense sensation she was experiencing. Did he feel it, too?

"Will you come for dinner?" she asked. This was the concession she'd intended to request. She wasn't quite sure why. She'd told herself it was so he'd be able to judge the way she handled the third task, which would expedite her introduction to John. But now...

He didn't answer.

"Please?"

He rubbed his thumb along hers and it was all Cassie could do not to faint. Her eyes drifted shut.

"I'll be there," he finally agreed.

"Thank you."

The argument between Frasier and Niles on the TV seemed to fade into the background. "I should go," she said.

"Yes," he said in a whisper. "You should." He released her and she clenched her fist to keep from grabbing his hand again.

"I'll see you at three o'clock on Sunday," she said hoarsely, staggering to her feet.

He nodded.

He didn't walk her to the door.

Chapter 12

Simon says: The perfect match lights a lasting fire.

Cassie pored over every cookbook she owned. They were all full of wonderful recipes. Even more encouraging, the instructions didn't seem too difficult. She had her menu set for this all-important dinner: roast turkey with a traditional stuffing, mashed potatoes and gravy, fresh green beans with butter and sliced almonds, two different salads and three kinds of pie, apple, pumpkin and pecan. Her grocery list was two pages long.

Angie had offered to help with the shopping; she'd also

volunteered to set the table. This was by far the most elaborate meal Cassie had ever undertaken.

Her brother, too, seemed eager to help. Luckily, Shawn was in town for a benefit and he'd promised to hand-letter the place cards. He said he'd also do small drawings on each, which were sure to be highly collectible—if any of her neighbors recognized her brother as the famous mural artist. Well, even if they didn't, they were bound to like the personal touch.

Reading over the stuffing recipe one last time, Cassie rested her elbows on the kitchen counter.

Unfortunately, her mind kept wandering from the page. She hadn't seen Simon since she'd visited him in his home. He'd fully recovered from his bout with the flu and gone back to work.

Cassie knew that because she'd phoned and chatted briefly with his assistant who'd told her Simon was indeed in the office. But when Ms. Snelling asked if Cassie wished to speak to him, she'd declined and hurriedly got off the phone.

Simon hadn't called to thank her for the soup, not that she expected him to. He was coming to dinner on Sunday and she almost dreaded seeing him; at the same time, she could hardly wait.

She hardly thought of John—John the engineer, John the perfect man—anymore. Only Simon seemed to inhabit her mind. And her heart?

Something was very wrong.

The doorbell rang and Cassie left her kitchen. Angie breezed into the room as though floating on air. This wasn't unusual these days. Her friend was in love. Angie seemed like a different person; nothing upset her, nothing annoyed her. In fact, she glowed with happiness. And yet she remained secretive about this new man in her life. Still, Cassie had begun to have her suspicions. In retrospect, the night of her solitary tree-decorating should have been a giveaway.

"You ready?" Angie asked.

"Shawn phoned earlier," Cassie said and carefully watched her friend's expression.

Angie revealed nothing.

"Oh, he's in town?"

"My brother seems to have a fair amount of business in the Pacific Northwest lately," Cassie said, playing along.

"He said he was here for some benefit, but if you ask me, the one who's benefiting is my brother."

Angie turned away and walked into the kitchen. She set down her purse, then removed her coat and draped it over the back of a kitchen chair. "This is your menu for tomorrow?" she said, still avoiding eye contact. She studied the paper on which Cassie had written her menu ideas. "Three different pies seems a bit ambitious, don't you think?"

"I wanted there to be choices." It didn't escape Cassie's notice how quickly Angie had diverted the subject from Shawn.

"Simon agreed to come, right?"

Switching the topic to Simon was a clever move. "Yes." Before she could expand or hint further about Shawn, the doorbell chimed again. Cassie opened the door to her brother, who hugged her enthusiastically. His eyes gleamed with a merriment that was due to more than the season, Cassie thought. When he saw Angie his expression sobered. He greeted her politely, even rather distantly.

"This dinner is becoming quite the affair," Shawn said, handing her the place cards. The artwork—small watercolors, all individual, of Christmas trees and bells and stars—was beautiful.

"Thanks!" Cassie kissed his cheek. "Okay, you two, sit down," she ordered. She indicated the sofa. "Before you say anything, I want you to know that I arranged for you to be here at the same time."

Shawn and Angie took opposite sides of the sofa while Cassie stood directly in front of them, her arms crossed. "You aren't fooling me, you know. I suspected the two of you were seeing each other."

"We wanted to tell you," Angie blurted out. "Well, I did, but Shawn felt we should wait."

"We weren't sure this was going anywhere," Shawn explained, glancing at Angie.

"We wanted to keep it to ourselves for a while," Angie said in a small voice, glancing back at Shawn.

"If you're upset, blame me," Shawn said, quick to defend Angie.

"Why wouldn't you want me to know?" Cassie asked, directing the question to both of them. "I'm happy for you!"

"It just kind of happened."

"We dated for a while a year ago after we met at your birthday party, and it didn't work out," Shawn said.

"For him, maybe, but it worked for me. I fell in love with Shawn." Angie looked down at her hands, which were neatly folded in her lap.

"Oh, my goodness!" Cassie brought one hand to her mouth. "Simon wouldn't take you on as a client because you were in love with someone else. That someone was my brother, wasn't it?"

Angie's ears turned red as she nodded. "Shawn and I went out last year, like he said, and just when everything seemed to be going well…I didn't hear from him."

"I was traveling a lot," he said. "A relationship's hard when I'm on the road so much. Besides, I was falling for Angie and it scared me. I'd dated plenty of women but I didn't feel about them the way I did about Angie—and I panicked."

"I was distraught when we broke up," Angie whispered. "I wanted to tell you, but Shawn—"

"You never said a word." Cassie was embarrassed that she'd been so oblivious. "Before *or* after you called it quits."

Angie shrugged apologetically.

"I like my privacy," Shawn said. "You know that."

Cassie couldn't help being a little hurt. "For crying out loud, I'm your sister."

"I'm sorry." Shawn did appear regretful. "Neither of us meant to offend you or anything."

"After we broke it off, I tried to move on," Angie said. "Which is why I agreed when my mother wanted me to meet the matchmaker."

"I made an effort to get over Angie, too," Shawn confessed, smiling at her, "but I couldn't get her out of my mind."

"Then we met again just before Thanksgiving."

"Here," Angie clarified. They both nodded.

"And I realized how much I'd missed Angie," he went on, "and how foolish I'd been to let our relationship end."

"And *I* realized that Simon was right and despite everything, I was still in love with Shawn."

They slid closer on the couch and Shawn took Angie's hand. They stared into each other's eyes.

Cassie wanted to kick them both for being so foolish, for not understanding what they had the first time around. They deserved a second kick for keeping it a secret from her.

"We've been so happy," Angie told her, "and I was afraid that if we said anything, you'd feel left out."

"Left out? If I feel left out it's because you guys—two

of the most important people in my life—didn't let me in on something as big as this!"

"We did plan to tell you," Angie said.

"And when would that have been?"

"After the big dinner party."

Cassie laughed. "So that's why it was so easy to convince you to make an appearance."

Shawn nodded. "Now that you know, we don't have to show up, do we? Angie and I have better things to do than attend this crazy dinner party of yours."

"Shawn," Angie chastised.

The hopeful expression on his face was enough to make Cassie laugh. "No, you two are excused. Angie, you don't need to help with the shopping."

"I'll come if you want," Angie said.

She would, too, but Cassie could see that she'd rather be alone with Shawn than spend the day in a crowded grocery store.

"I'll be fine. Do something productive with your time, though—like shopping for an engagement ring."

Angie blushed again and Shawn cleared his throat. "As it happens, I have a ring picked out."

"You do?" Angie asked with tears in her voice.

"I'm not letting you get away from me again," Shawn said. "There's still plenty to discuss, but I can't see—"

"Yes."

"Yes, what?" he asked.

"Yes, I'll marry you and, yes, there's a lot still to be decided. But there's no obstacle the two of us can't overcome."

They left a few minutes later, so in love they couldn't keep their hands off each other.

Cassie had difficulty wiping the grin off her face. Shawn and Angie were perfect together. She wondered why she hadn't thought of it before—or noticed what was going on. Angie would probably move away from Seattle once they were married, which was the only disadvantage to an otherwise ideal situation.

All of a sudden it became crucial to talk to Simon. She had his office number and as she suspected he had an answering service.

"Would you please ask Mr. Dodson to return my call? It's…an emergency."

She didn't have to wait long for him to call back. When his name flashed across caller ID, Cassie exhaled a huge sigh of relief.

"Simon?" she said.

"Yes."

Cassie smiled at his gruff, unfriendly tone. She felt better already.

"There's been a change in our dinner plans."

"That's why you phoned?"

"Yes. My brother and Angie won't be attending."

"That's your emergency?'

"This might not be earth-shattering to you but—"

"Cassie…"

"I knew they were secretly involved, or at least I guessed they were. It's wonderful for them. They make a fabulous couple. I couldn't be happier, even if it means I'm going to lose my best friend."

Her outburst was followed by a short silence. "I don't quite understand why you called me. And I suggest you think of it as gaining a sister-in-law," he advised wryly, "not losing a friend."

"Yes, that's true, but she'll leave Seattle and the lab.… Anyway," she said in a more cheerful voice, "I wanted to let you know you were right about her being in love."

"Of course I was right. Did you seriously doubt it?"

"Well, perhaps not." She paused. "I shouldn't have called. You must consider me a nuisance."

"We can agree on that," he murmured.

"I know you regret taking me on as a client and I apologize for being such a pest."

"I've dealt with worse clients."

Funny how reassuring Cassie found even that faint encouragement.

He exhaled slowly. "You're upset. Is it because of your friend and your brother? Anything that upsets the status quo—even a good thing like this—takes time to accept."

Cassie wasn't sure why she'd felt such an overwhelming urge to hear his voice. His certainty was comforting, she supposed. He always had an answer, a reason, a solution.

"How can I help?" he asked, his tone almost gentle.

"I…I don't know."

"I have an idea," he said, his voice brightening.

"What?"

"I'll tell you something else about John."

"John?"

"The man I've matched you with."

"Oh. Yes." The man she'd paid thirty thousand dollars to meet. He'd completely slipped her mind.

"Okay," he said. "Let me think about it."

"What were you doing?" She felt guilty at the thought of interrupting him. "Before I called."

"What was I doing?" he repeated. "Why do you ask?"

"If I'm being too much of a bother, I'll hang up." She viewed him as someone who operated with purpose. Someone whose day was filled with constant demands. He had too many responsibilities to be interrupted by such mundane matters as her doubts and insecurities.

"I'm watching a college football game."

"You watch football?" He couldn't have shocked her more had he said he was on an aircraft headed for the moon. Practically every day Simon surprised her with how...*human* he was.

"Why would you find that unusual?"

"I didn't think football would interest you. It's so...so normal."

He laughed. "I am normal, Cassie. I'm like every other man."

"No, you aren't," she insisted. "You aren't like any other man I've ever known, and now I'm seeing this whole other side of you and it's confusing."

He muttered something under his breath; it sounded as

if he'd said he was confused himself, but Cassie couldn't be sure of that.

"About John," he said, changing the subject.

"I don't want to hear about John right now."

"Maybe you should. It'll adjust your focus."

"No, thanks. I'll be meeting him soon, won't I?"

"I can arrange the meeting for Monday afternoon if you like. When I last spoke to him about scheduling a face-to-face, John was ecstatic. He's *very* eager to make your acquaintance."

"Oh."

"He called it an early Christmas gift."

"Oh, yes, Christmas."

Silence stretched between them.

"I'll get to your condo a few minutes early," Simon said, filling the empty space. "I have your address. From your application—and the check."

The thirty-thousand-dollar check…

"See you then," he added.

"Yes, for dinner." Not until she'd hung up her phone, did she wonder why he wanted to come early.

Chapter 13

Cassie was up half the night baking pies and getting everything ready for her final task. Her alarm went off at six on Sunday morning. She staggered from her bed, got the turkey out of the refrigerator and nearly dropped it on the kitchen floor. Who knew twenty pounds would be so heavy?

Because she'd methodically planned every detail of the dinner preparations, she was right on schedule. She stuffed the turkey and it was in the oven and roasting nicely an hour later. She started on the salads next. The dining room table was set with a crisp white linen cloth. There were sprigs of holly beside each place card for a festive accent. She'd arranged every detail with the hope of impressing Simon. She'd dressed in a red and black velvet pantsuit and taken care with her makeup. For a final holiday touch she wore a ring with a large red stone.

He arrived a full hour before her guests were due, carrying a huge, perfect poinsettia for the centerpiece.

He handed it to her almost as if he was grateful to be rid of it.

"How lovely," she said delightedly. "Thank you."

She put the poinsettia on the table and stepped back to examine it.

"I love it, Simon." Rising onto the tips of her toes, she kissed his cheek.

He was frowning when she stepped back. "That was inappropriate," he said disapprovingly.

She didn't point out that he'd kissed her a few weeks ago. But to prove how wrong he was, she kissed his cheek a second time.

However, when she started to move away, Simon clasped her by the shoulders and pulled her into his embrace. Then he lowered his mouth to hers. Before she could account for her response, she threw her arms around his neck and kissed him back.

They both seemed to realize at precisely the same moment what they'd done. They leaped apart; Simon shoved his hands in his pockets, while Cassie turned around in an effort to regain her composure.

As they faced each other again, Cassie made a sweeping gesture toward the table, hoping to bring some levity to the situation. "Well, what do you think?" she asked.

He nodded. "You've done a wonderful job."

"Would you like to see the turkey?" she asked.

"If you wish."

"I do. You're the one who told me I had to do this… and in retrospect I'm glad you did." She led him into the kitchen, grabbed one of her oven mitts and opened the door. She basted the turkey and noted with pride how crisp and brown it looked. According to her calculations, it would be finished in forty minutes. Simon could remove it from the oven and it would sit for an additional fifteen minutes before being carved.

"Very nice," he said, when she closed the oven door. "Smells delicious, too."

"Have I surprised you?" she asked and knew she had, which was what she'd hoped.

He smiled. "I admit that you're one surprise after another." Which was exactly the thought she'd so recently had about him....

She managed to restrain herself from dancing a small, gleeful jig.

She poured Simon a glass of eggnog while they waited for the rest of her company. "Store-bought," she confessed as she joined him in the living room. They sat on opposite ends of the sofa.

That wasn't the only similarity to the way Shawn and Angie had behaved the previous day. Like her brother and her friend, Simon and Cassie hardly looked at each other. Neither seemed inclined toward conversation, either.

"I was thinking..." Cassie began.

"It seems to me..." Simon said.

They both stopped, then Simon gestured toward her to speak.

"No, you first," she insisted.

"Please," he said.

Cassie didn't get a chance because the doorbell rang just then. Eager to break the unexplained tension between them, she hurried to answer. As she might have guessed, Mrs. Mullinex arrived first. She stood in the hallway dressed in her finest. For the first time in Cassie's memory, her hair wasn't in curlers. In fact, this was the first time she'd seen her neighbor's hair, period. It was…curly.

"This is so nice of you," the older woman chirped. Her eyes flew instantly to Simon and widened with womanly appreciation.

"This is…" Cassie wasn't sure how to introduce him. "Simon. My friend. Simon Dodson, Mrs. Mullinex."

"How do you do?" her neighbor cooed sweetly. "Please call me Phyllis."

"Phyllis," Cassie repeated. She'd lived in the building for three years and hadn't been aware of Mrs. Mullinex's first name, which didn't appear on the mailbox, not even as an initial. Her neighbor had never seen fit to share it with Cassie.

"I didn't realize Cassie had a male friend," Mrs. Mullinex said ever so coyly. "She is a sly one."

Cassie excused herself and disappeared inside the kitchen while she prepared the hors d'oeuvres. She'd leave Simon to fend for himself. When she heard the two of them chatting amicably, Cassie sighed. Simon possessed a few social graces, after all—but none that he was willing to display for *her* benefit.

Mr. Oliver showed up next. "The Seahawks game starts at four. This isn't going to take longer than that, is it?" he asked as he barreled past her and into the condo. He looked around and when he saw Phyllis Mullinex, a frown darkened his face.

"Mr. Oliver," Mrs. Mullinex greeted him stiffly.

"Phyllis."

They glared at each other like alley cats with hackles raised, each waiting for the other to make the first move.

"So...you two know each other," Cassie commented, watching them carefully.

"No," said Mrs. Mullinex.

"Oh, yes, we know each other very well," Mr. Oliver countered. "Would you mind if I turned the TV on?" he asked as he claimed the most comfortable chair. Not waiting for a response, he reached for the remote, leaned forward and pressed the on button. The television screen lit up and he immediately found the station he wanted. It featured another football game—not the Seahawks.

"I'd like to introduce my friend Dr. Simon Dodson,"

Cassie said, speaking loudly enough to be heard above the roar of the sports announcer.

Mr. Oliver acknowledged Simon with a disinterested nod of his head.

Her doorbell rang again. Grateful for an excuse to escape, Cassie rushed forward to answer. Bob, the rap aficionado from next door, stood on the other side. He'd apparently gone to some effort with his appearance; he'd greased his graying hair back from his forehead and donned a fresh pair of jeans and a sweater. He grinned when he saw her and handed her a lone rose.

"Welcome," Cassie said and brought him into the room.

When he saw the others, Bob's face fell. "You didn't say there'd be anyone else here," he said.

"Oh...sorry. I assumed you knew."

"So, dinner isn't just for the two of us?"

"Ah...no. I'm sure you've met Mrs. Mullinex and Mr. Oliver," Cassie said, motioning toward her guests.

"No, and I don't particularly care to," he grumbled.

"This is my friend Dr. Simon Dodson."

Bob's frown deepened. "You have a...friend?"

"Well, yes, sort of." The last thing she needed was for

Bob to think she was interested in his attentions. If avoiding *that* trap meant stretching the truth, then so be it.

The oven timer went off, and Cassie took the opportunity to leave and close the kitchen door behind her. After all her hard work, this meal was going to be a disaster. None of these people liked one another.

Simon followed her into the kitchen. "Should the turkey come out yet?" he asked.

"Yes," she said distractedly as he slipped his hands into her Santa-face oven mitts.

"Simon," she pleaded. "What are we going to do?"

"About what?"

"Can't you see?" she cried. "Mrs. Mullinex and Mr. Oliver can barely stand to look at each other, and Bob thought this dinner was going to be a private affair between him and me."

"It'll be fine," he said soothingly.

Cassie sincerely doubted that.

Simon lifted the turkey out of the oven and set it on top of the stove.

Cassie thanked him. "According to my cookbook, the turkey should sit for no less than fifteen minutes before being carved."

"Do you need help with anything else?"

"No." She'd seen to everything before the guests were due. "I just have to get the food into the serving dishes."

Bowls lined the counter. Cassie was pleased with her organizational abilities. The potatoes were cooked and ready to be mashed. Green beans simmered on the stove-top. She drained off the liquid, added the melted butter and almonds and placed them in the bowl she'd chosen.

Simon returned to the living room with the others.

Then, picking up the bowl in which she planned to put the stuffing, she noticed something wrong. For a moment, all Cassie could do was stare at her hand.

No! Oh, dear. Now what?

Putting down the bowl, she opened the door slightly and peered out of the kitchen. "Simon," she called in a deceptively casual voice. "Would you come in here for a minute?"

He gave her an odd look but did as she requested.

The instant he set foot in the kitchen, she took his arms and pulled him all the way in. "Houston, we have a problem," she said in an urgent whisper.

"What kind of problem?"

"A very big one." Splaying her fingers, she held out her hand. "My ring is missing."

"Your ring."

"Yes, my ring."

He seemed unconcerned. "I'm sure it's around here somewhere. Can't you look for it later?"

"No."

"And why not?" he asked.

"Because the last time I saw it, I was stuffing the turkey."

"In other words…"

"Yes. In other words it's inside the bird."

"You're positive?"

"No, but where else would it be?"

Simon rolled his eyes toward the ceiling.

"What am I going to do?" A dozen scenarios played in her mind, none of them the least bit amusing. If someone bit into it and broke a tooth… "I'll be sued!" she said hoarsely, covering her eyes. "Someone might choke on it. My neighbors don't deserve to die, even if my newspapers do turn up missing now and then."

"Dish the stuffing into the bowl. You might find it."

"Okay, okay."

"And don't panic."

"Easy for you to say," she muttered as she transferred stuffing into the bowl, inspecting each spoonful closely.

"Mrs. Mullinex is a sweet lady," he was saying. "I don't know why you think she'd want to cause you any trouble."

"And Mr. Oliver?"

"He probably wouldn't even notice if he bit into the ring, especially if you left the football game on."

"And Bob?"

"He'd assume you were proposing marriage."

"Very funny."

"Oh, Cassie, I just—"

Mrs. Mullinex stuck her head into the kitchen. "Anything I can do, dear?"

"Ah, no, thanks. Everything's fine," Cassie assured her.

"Simon, come back and sit with me," the older woman wheedled.

Simon turned away from the counter and offered Mrs. Mullinex his arm, then threw Cassie a look that told her she was on her own.

A lot of help *he'd* been.

No sooner had Simon left than the door opened again. This time it was Bob.

"So," he said, leaning against the kitchen counter. "It's just the two of us now."

"Yes, well..." Cassie inserted the spoon inside the turkey to finish taking out the stuffing, but with Bob watching every move, she couldn't make a huge production of plowing through it, searching for her ring.

"I've always loved stuffing."

"Oh, me, too, but I'm not sure this turned out that well. I was thinking I wouldn't serve it."

"Let me taste." Before she could protest, he took her spoon and helped himself to a sample. After blowing on it, he popped it into his mouth. He smiled widely in approval. "This is fabulous! The best I've ever tasted."

"You're just being kind."

"Not at all. Here, I'll take it out for you."

"No," she cried and made an effort to stop him, but to no avail. Bob carried the bowl into the dining area.

When she followed with the salads, she saw that he'd taken a forkful to Mrs. Mullinex. "Cassie says the stuffing didn't turn out to her liking. I disagree. What do you think?"

Mrs. Mullinex gave it a dainty taste. "Perfection," she said. "You're being modest, Cassie."

Mr. Oliver stood. "What's a turkey dinner without stuffing?"

"I didn't want to ruin anyone's diet," Cassie said, searching for an excuse, any excuse, to get the stuffing off the table.

Mr. Oliver raised his hand. "I'm on a low-carb diet myself."

"Then you won't want any of the stuffing," Cassie said thankfully.

"I thought I'd make an exception, this being Christmas and all."

"Oh…"

"Let's all help," Mrs. Mullinex suggested cheerfully. "We can bring out the rest of the serving dishes. We shouldn't leave all the work to Cassie."

Cassie sent a pleading glance in Simon's direction. He, however, was looking elsewhere.

Chapter 14

Simon says: A good matchmaker stays in the background, just like Santa's little helper, then swoops in at the opportune moment.

Cassie couldn't swallow a single bite as she carefully studied her guests enjoying their turkey with all the trimmings. Every time she saw a forkful of stuffing heading toward someone's mouth she had to restrain herself from leaping to her feet and yanking it away.

Simon revealed no such concern. Mrs. Mullinex had him engaged in a lengthy conversation. Judging by the attention he paid her, anyone would think she was the wittiest, prettiest woman on the face of the earth. Every once in a while, the older woman released a girlish trill that sounded, to Cassie's somewhat jaundiced ear, like a songbird strangling on too much seed.

"Mighty fine dinner," Bob told Cassie, eyeing her with far more appreciation than his meal.

"Thank you." She quickly looked away and offered Mr. Oliver more beans. More salad. More anything.

"Do you always cook like this?" Mr. Oliver asked. Before she could answer, he continued. "You probably have plenty of leftovers. No need to let 'em go to waste."

"That'd be a shame," Bob threw in. "I'd be happy to come over and help you finish them a few times a week."

Cassie felt it was important to set *him* straight right away. "Since I work and there's only me to cook for, I generally don't go to this much trouble." *Generally—like never!*

Bob glanced at Mr. Oliver, whose plate was heaped high with large portions of mashed potatoes and gravy. "I thought you said you were watching your weight?"

"Low-carb's the only way to go." He reached across the table for the butter, which he slathered on a roll.

"Cassie, dear," Mrs. Mullinex said in the same high-pitched bird voice she'd used since meeting Simon. "It's been such a long time since I made gravy. Does yours always have these lumps in it?"

Cassie stiffened her shoulders at the frightening thought that the ring might have slipped into the gravy. Then she realized her neighbor was denigrating her gravy-making skills, although she wasn't sure why. Her gravy was flawless, and if there were any lumps, which there weren't, it was a fluke. "No, I added them for your benefit," she answered in an equally saccharine voice.

Simon's gaze narrowed.

"Oh." Mrs. Mullinex blinked as if gauging whether or not to be offended.

"I'm joking, Mrs. Mullinex," Cassie said, feeling slightly guilty. "I apologize if there are lumps in the gravy."

"You can put lumps in my gravy anytime you want," Bob told her. He winked at her, then jiggled his eyebrows. Disgusting! The man was old enough to be her father.

"I believe I'll have some more of that stuffing," Simon said.

Cassie sprang from her chair and grabbed hold of the bowl. "I was going to take it back to the kitchen."

"Gimme that when you're finished," Mr. Oliver said, grinning broadly.

"Ah..." Cassie looked helplessly at Simon, who gently pried the bowl from her hands. "I'm not sure there's enough."

"There's plenty for everyone," Simon said and took a huge spoonful before passing it across the table to Mr. Oliver. "Let me hand it around."

"Doesn't anyone want to save room for pie?" Cassie asked brightly. She described each one, highlighting the fine qualities of the apple, pumpkin and pecan fillings.

"I don't know if I dare," Mrs. Mullinex trilled. "One must watch one's waistline." She paused, gazing around as if waiting for someone to tell her she needn't worry about such things.

Cassie volunteered in the hope that if her neighbor accepted the pie, she'd skip the extra stuffing, which, to her horror, was being passed around the table. "Why, Mrs. Mullinex, you have a very good figure."

"Pleasingly plump," Bob seconded.

The smile faded from the other woman's face. "Plump?"

"*Pleasingly* plump," Cassie said. "That's another way of saying—"

"I'm fat," Mrs. Mullinex cut in, frowning now.

"I like to be direct," Mr. Oliver said, glaring at the older woman. "Plump is plump, no matter how you try to fancy it up."

"Leave it to you to insult me, Harry," she snapped.

"You always were quick to take offense," Mr. Oliver snapped back. "A man makes a simple comment and you jump all over him and ruin a perfectly fine friendship."

"Ah..." Cassie raised her index finger, trying to get a comment in before the confrontation broke into a full-fledged argument.

"I don't know how anyone could even imply that you're overweight," Simon said, pouring everyone a little more wine.

Cassie managed a smile at his smooth handling of what was rapidly becoming an awkward situation. It also gave her an opportunity to make off with the stuffing unobserved.

"I'll put on a pot of coffee," Cassie said, jumping up from the table. She grabbed the stuffing bowl and practically ran into the kitchen, convinced she was about to have a nervous breakdown. Once inside, she leaned against the wall and breathed deeply, wanting nothing more than this dinner to be over.

When she returned, Simon had collected the dinner plates. Cassie reached for the gravy boat and stared down at it. Lumps, indeed! She couldn't find a single one!

Thankfully, after coffee and dessert, Cassie started to relax. Again Mrs. Mullinex damned her with faint praise regarding the pie, but by then Cassie didn't care. Besides, she had to agree—the apples were unevenly sliced.

"Don't you have anything good to say?" Mr. Oliver muttered. "I thought the pies were great. All of 'em."

"Excellent meal," Bob told her and tried to take her hand.

Cassie snatched it away before he had the chance. As far as she was concerned, the man should be arrested.

"I'll have you know, *Mr.* Oliver, I've paid Cassie several compliments," Mrs. Mullinex said righteously.

If that was the case, they'd flown right over Cassie's head.

By the time she saw her last neighbor to the door, Cassie was exhausted. As soon as Bob left—with obvious reluctance—she collapsed into a chair.

"You look a bit out of sorts," Simon commented.

"You think?" The man had mastered the art of understatement.

He grinned and sat on the sofa across from her. "Actually, the meal went well."

"You have got to be kidding. It was a disaster!"

"You're being too hard on yourself. You did an admirable job, and while it might not seem that your neighbors fully appreciated what you did, I believe they had an enjoyable afternoon."

She gave him a weak smile. "I don't know if I should be glad the ring didn't show up or not."

"Is it valuable?"

"Not really. I bought it in Hawaii a few years back. I hate to lose it, though." She raised her shoulders in a shrug. "But if it hasn't turned up by now, I doubt it ever will. For all I know, it might be in Mr. Oliver's digestive system."

"I'm sure it's not."

"What makes you say that?"

Reaching inside his suit pocket, Simon pulled out the ring, displaying it proudly between index finger and thumb. "Is this the ring you misplaced?"

Speechless, all Cassie could do was stare at him. Once the shock wore off, she lunged forward and grabbed the ring. "You're telling me you found it?"

"I did."

"Where?"

"On the kitchen counter. You must've taken it off and forgotten. I tried to get your attention in the kitchen and then at dinner but you ignored me."

"I didn't take it off." Cassie would've remembered that.

"Then it must have fallen off before you stuffed the turkey."

Cassie held the ring in one cupped hand, her relief overwhelming. Then, slowly, her suspicions started to rise. "Exactly when did you find this?"

"Just before Phyllis came into the kitchen. As I said, I tried to tell you but you were too flustered to notice."

"Phyllis?" she echoed. "Mrs. Mullinex is now Phyllis to you?"

"She's a delightful mature woman."

"Hmm. Then again, she isn't stealing *your* newspapers."

"I suggest you purchase her a subscription for Christmas."

"I'll think about it," Cassie muttered. Then, remembering the ring, she glared at him. "That was cruel and unusual punishment, letting me worry that someone was going to swallow this ring."

"I *tried* to tell you I'd found it," Simon said in his own defense. "Why else do you think I was passing the stuffing around?"

Well, there was that. "I'm too tired to argue with you." She stretched her legs out and let her hands dangle at her sides. Unable to prevent it, she yawned.

Taking that as his cue to leave, Simon stood. "I'd better go."

Cassie realized with a start that she wanted him to stay. "Don't go yet," she urged.

"Do you want help with the cleanup?"

"No."

"A drink or more coffee?"

She shook her head. "There's a football game on," she said.

Cassie could see he was tempted. Smiling up at him, she hoped that was enough incentive to get him to change his mind.

"I should get home," he finally said.

"Why?"

"I just should. And don't forget I'll be seeing you tomorrow," he reminded her.

"Tomorrow?"

"In my office. Late afternoon."

She couldn't recall an appointment, but if they had one, she'd certainly keep it.

"John will be there."

Oh, my goodness. Cassie had forgotten she was supposed to meet John. "Cancel it," she said hurriedly.

Simon frowned.

"I'm not ready to meet John."

"You've completed your three tasks to my satisfaction. I don't understand why you're hesitating. You've worked hard and waited for quite a while, and so has John. I hate to disappoint him."

Cassie's head was spinning with doubt and fear. "I need to talk to you first."

"Talk to me now," he said, none too patiently.

"I can't—I'm tired, and besides, I...I need to think."

He continued to frown, and she could see he wasn't happy with her. He left soon after.

Cassie sat on the sofa for at least an hour, trying to

make sense of her relationship with Simon. Her feelings for him and her original expectations of John were scrambled in her mind. Eventually, when her whole life felt like a hopeless tangle, she called Angie.

Thankfully her friend was home.

"I need help," Cassie whispered.

"Cassie?" Angie said. "What's wrong?"

"I've done something foolish."

"What?"

She said the words out loud for the very first time. "I've fallen in love with Simon."

Chapter 15

Simon says: There's a perfect match for you; it just isn't me.

By the time Cassie reached Simon's office, she'd worked everything out. She'd rehearsed her speech all day. Her one hope was that Simon would own up to the fact that he shared her feelings.

His assistant greeted her warmly. "Hello, Ms. Beaumont. It's good to see you again."

"You, too, Ms. Snelling. Oh, nice tree."

That was the extent of the Christmas decorating in

Simon's office—a small Norfolk pine on the credenza, draped with tiny white lights. Simple, classy, elegant.

Given her previous experiences visiting his office, Cassie automatically took a seat and picked up a magazine.

"Dr. Dodson will see you now."

"Already?"

"Yes, he told me I was to bring you into his office as soon as you arrived."

Cassie set the magazine aside and stood. It was now or never. The only thing left to do was forge ahead and pray they could discuss this with openness and honesty.

Ms. Snelling held the door for her. "Ms. Beaumont," she said, announcing Cassie.

As he had at their first meeting, Simon sat behind his desk, studying a periodical. He glanced up, acknowledging her with a nod, then resumed reading.

Cassie took a seat, crossed her legs, uncrossed them, then folded her hands as she waited. She knew Simon now and was familiar with his ways.

When he did finally look up, Cassie could see that he was on edge. She wondered if he'd managed to sleep after he'd left her apartment and suspected he'd tossed and turned, the same as she had.

"You said you wanted to speak to me." His voice was expressionless.

"Yes, please."

He checked his watch. "You have ten minutes."

That dictatorial approach didn't fool her. He wasn't going to intimidate her, nor was he going to scare her into being silent.

"Ten minutes," she said softly. "I doubt it'll take that long."

He leaned back and Cassie leaned forward. "If you'll recall, it was my friend Angie who suggested I make an appointment with you."

He indicated with a slight nod that he remembered.

"You turned her down, right?"

"Yes." He sounded bored. "You know very well I did."

"For an excellent reason," she said, "as you and I are both aware."

He checked his watch again, as if to point out that the minutes were ticking away.

"Even though you rejected her, Angie thought highly enough of your skills as a matchmaker to recommend you to me."

"I know my business, Cassie."

"You won't get any argument from me." She grinned and looked down at her hands, surprised by how calm and controlled she sounded. While her heart continued to beat at an accelerated rate, she remained outwardly collected. "At first I thought the idea of those three tasks was ridiculous, but I complied. In fact, I was willing to do just about anything to prove my value as a wife."

Once more he glanced at his watch.

"I understand now why you chose the tasks you did. Each one served a specific purpose. You knew all the facts I could list on a sheet of paper, and as a psychologist you could discern a great deal from that, but you didn't know the real me." She'd given much thought to his motives. "You didn't know my heart."

"Yes, well..."

"You wanted to find out how I interact with strangers as a volunteer. You wanted to see how well I deal with children and then you were interested in my homemaking skills."

"Practical aspects of any good marriage. But these tasks also told me that you have compassion and flexibility and a sense of humor."

She bowed her head to hide her pleasure at his words.

"John is looking for a woman who's willing to have children with him. A woman who enjoys socializing and wants to be part of a community. You are all those things."

He'd introduced the subject of John, so she'd better get that out of the way right now. "Oh, yes. John, the match you chose on my behalf. I do hope you cancelled the appointment."

"Per your request I did. However, I feel you should know John was extremely disappointed, as I expected he would be."

"I would've been, too, if I'd been waiting to meet my perfect match. Or as you'd probably say, my most *suitable* match," she said with a grin.

"And you aren't?" Simon challenged.

"No, unfortunately I've already made his acquaintance."

Simon's eyes narrowed. "Before you say anything else, I want you to think this through very carefully."

"I have," she said.

"I beg to differ." Simon spoke in the same unfriendly tones she'd heard at the beginning of their relationship.

"I brought up Angie's name for a specific reason. You knew after reading her answers to your questionnaire, and during your initial meeting, that she was in love with someone else." She paused. "As I told you on Saturday, that someone happens to be my brother. As I also told you, I was impressed by your insight in recognizing her feelings for Shawn so easily."

"As I've repeatedly said, I'm good at my job."

"You knew it would be wrong to introduce her to another man when she loved my brother."

"Yes."

"It would be just as wrong to introduce me to John when I'm in love with...you."

Simon briefly closed his eyes, then stood. "I've said it before and I'll say it again. Don't do this, Cassie. I'm off-limits."

"I can't keep still. I wish I could, but I can't."

He reclaimed his seat. Looking exasperated, he informed her, "This happens far more often than you realize. I've lost count of the number of women who believe they've fallen in love with me."

"I'm sure that's true." Simon was an attractive man. He had a strong sensual appeal and would turn heads wherever he went. She didn't assume for an instant that she was the only woman ever to fall for him.

"The thing you seem to forget is that you've paid thirty thousand dollars to meet the man I've chosen as your match."

Cassie hadn't forgotten.

"I held up my part of the bargain," he said.

"Yes, you did."

"I've deposited the check and it's cleared your bank."

She nodded.

"If you voluntarily decide not to meet your match, you should know there'll be no refund."

"I didn't think there would be."

"If you walk away now, without meeting John, you'll forfeit your money." He said it again, as if he felt it necessary to remind her of what was at risk.

"I'm aware of that."

"It would be foolish for you to do this."

"I've been called a fool for lesser things," she said calmly.

He shook his head. "I wouldn't have expected you to be an unreasonable woman."

"Really?" She smiled, just a little.

He looked pointedly at his watch. "Your time's about up. Is there anything else you'd care to say…in closing?"

This last part was said with emphasis, as though he was eager to usher her out the door.

"I'm almost finished," she told him.

He sighed.

"I'm not telling you how I feel so you can laugh at me, Simon."

His gaze held hers. "I would never do that," he said, then added, "any more than I did with the other women."

She tried to disguise a smile. "Nor do I wish to be humiliated."

He agreed with a nod.

"I have reason to believe you share my feelings."

"You—"

"Do you kiss other female clients?" she asked, interrupting him.

He was silent.

"I didn't think so. How many have you taken to your home?"

"None," he admitted from between clenched teeth.

"That's what I thought," she said. To her relief, he was being honest.

"I've never had a woman...a client break down in tears and turn to me for comfort. Yes, I stepped over the line. I regretted it immediately and, if you recall, I apologized."

"You did."

"I realized it was a mistake to allow any client access to my personal life after you showed up at my home later with the soup. I should never have invited you inside."

"Why did you?"

He refused to meet her eyes. "I'd been ill for several days and my resistance was weak."

"Resistance to me?"

"No," he countered sharply, "resistance to impropriety."

"Ah." So that was the excuse he'd chosen.

"Afterward, I was afraid you might have read more into that evening than was warranted, and I see now that you have. I'm sorry I didn't address the subject earlier. I wish I had. As I feared, you've got the wrong impression."

"I see."

"It would be best if we could forget that evening entirely, put it out of our minds."

"I'm sorry," she said. "I can't forget that night. I can't make myself regret it, either. It was after our evening together that I knew, Simon. I'd fallen in love with you."

Simon met her look unflinchingly and yielded no

emotion. "Please don't continue. This is embarrassing for you *and* for me."

"I have one other comment," she said, striving to remain unemotional. "Actually, it's more of a question than a comment."

"Then out with it, and let this matter be laid to rest."

She thanked him with a brief nod. "I can accept that a distraught female weeping on your shoulder might have caused you to offer comfort in a way you normally wouldn't."

"Thank you. I appreciate your understanding."

"I can even accept the fact that your resistance was low when I dropped by your home that evening."

Once more he nodded.

"But how do you account for the way you kissed me on Sunday?"

"Sunday?" he repeated. The color seemed to drain from his face.

"Can you tell me what prompted that kiss?" she asked.

He didn't answer for a long moment. "I have no excuse," he finally said.

"I'm not looking for excuses, Simon, I'm looking for honesty. It hasn't been easy to lay out my heart for you.

If I've misread the situation, then I apologize. In that case, I'll walk out your door right now and you'll never hear from me again."

"That would...be a shame."

"Yes, it would," she agreed, hope seeping in for the first time since she'd entered his office.

"You've paid me a lot of money and I'd feel bad if you allowed this opportunity to slip by. John is awaiting an introduction, and I hate to disappoint him."

Cassie closed her eyes, struggling to hold on to her poise. After a moment, she opened them and met his look head-on. "I'm not meeting John or any other man you deem the right mate for me. Or my 'suitable' mate or whatever word you want to use. I've already found him and it's you."

Simon didn't acknowledge that comment in any way.

"*Have* I misread your feelings, Simon?" she asked softly.

He refused to answer.

Reluctantly she stood; she'd gone past her allotted ten minutes. "I won't embarrass you further—or myself for that matter. But before I go, I have one simple request."

"Fine," he said tersely.

"Look me in the eyes and tell me you don't love me. Do that and I'll leave and never trouble you again."

"I'm not playing word games with you, Cassie."

"This isn't a game. It's my life, my future—our future."

He squinted up at the ceiling. "Why do women have such a flair for the dramatic? I suppose you're going to spend the rest of your life pining away for me."

"No, I won't," she told him. "I love you and it's up to you to accept or reject that love. It'll hurt me, but I know I'll get over you in time. In every likelihood I'll marry someone else one day and perhaps even have children. Rest assured that if you reject me, I won't leap off a bridge."

"That's a relief."

She moved away from the chair, her heart pounding so hard she was astonished it didn't echo through the room. She gave him ample opportunity to stop her.

He didn't.

With her hand on the door, she turned back to look at Simon one last time. He sat at his desk, reading. She wasn't fooled. He might not admit it, but he loved her.

"Merry Christmas, Simon."

He glanced up and his eyes flared as though he was surprised to see her still in the room. "Oh. Merry Christmas."

"Goodbye."

She didn't wait for a response. Head held high, she marched out the door. Once on the other side, she closed her eyes, almost collapsing to the floor as a wave of deep loss hit her.

Ms. Snelling's chair scraped as she stood. "Oh, dear. Are you all right, Ms. Beaumont? You look like you're about to faint."

"I—I'm okay," she stammered. "Thank you...." she added politely.

It was exactly as Cassie had feared. Simon Dodson, professional matchmaker, was an expert at finding love for everyone except himself.

Chapter 16

"Hold the elevator!" Cassie shouted, rushing across the condo foyer on Wednesday afternoon. When she saw that the lone occupant was Mr. Oliver, she automatically slowed her steps. No need to rush; he'd take sadistic delight in letting the doors shut in her face. To her amazement, he thrust out his arm and stopped them from closing.

Cassie hardly knew what to think. "Thank you," she managed as she hurried into the elevator, loaded down with her mail, the newspaper, her purse and a couple of last-minute Christmas purchases.

The newspaper.

She hadn't even realized Mrs. Mullinex hadn't "borrowed" it since their dinner together. That was progress.

"My pleasure," Mr. Oliver said as the elevator doors glided shut. "Can't thank you enough for the great dinner."

It seemed wrong to confess that if it hadn't been for Simon she would never have thought to invite Mr. Oliver.

Try as she might, she couldn't get Simon out of her mind. She'd given it her best shot, told him how she felt and done what she could to convince him that he shared her feelings. But she hadn't expected the strength of his conviction in denying his love for her. Nor could she understand why he fought it so hard.

What bothered her most was his inability to admit to her face that he didn't love her. If he had, she might have believed him. However, for reasons she'd likely never know, he refused to accept her love.

"Nice young man..."

"I'm sorry," Cassie said. "I didn't catch what you said?"

"That Simon of yours. He's a fine young man. You've chosen well."

"I...thank you," she whispered. No need to explain that he wasn't "hers," or that she wouldn't be seeing him again. Cassie had been sincere when she'd told him she wouldn't pine away for the rest of her life. He'd made his decision and she'd made hers.

The elevator stopped, and Mr. Oliver held the door for her to exit first. When they stepped into the hallway, Mrs. Mullinex opened her condo door and, seeing the two of them, waved cheerfully. Cassie noticed that the other woman's eyes immediately went to Harry Oliver.

"Oh, what perfect timing," Phyllis said. Her hair was brushed into soft waves and she looked lovely.

"Good afternoon, Harry," she purred.

"Hello, Phyllis."

Cassie hid a satisfied grin. Apparently there'd been a breakthrough in that relationship. Wonderful!

"I was hoping to see you," she said, smiling shyly at Harry. "I thought I'd invite my dearest friends over for eggnog on Christmas Eve. I do hope you can join me." As if she realized she'd directed the invitation solely to Mr. Oliver, she turned to Cassie. "I'd like it if you could come, too."

"Why...thank you, I'd be honored." Cassie's brother

and Angie had invited her to spend Christmas Day with Angie's family. They'd been generous to include her, and Cassie had gratefully accepted.

"I wonder..." Phyllis began. "If you'd like to invite your young man, please do. That Simon is quite the charmer."

She nodded. "I'll mention it if I talk to him between now and Christmas Eve." That was highly improbable, but again she didn't feel it was necessary to go into details.

"Why wouldn't you be talking to him?" Mrs. Mullinex pressed. "'Tis the season and he's your sweetheart."

Cassie glanced away. "Actually, he isn't."

"You don't mean that!"

"They might've had a spat," Harry suggested.

"In that case, dear, I urge you to settle it before Christmas." She looked at Harry and blushed. "Don't let too much time elapse before you set things right."

Harry stepped closer to Phyllis. "I couldn't agree with you more."

Rather than tell them there was nothing to settle, Cassie just thanked them for their advice.

They made an arrangement to meet, and Cassie let herself into her condo. The festive cheer of the season greeted her, and for a moment all she could do was stand and stare at her Christmas tree and the other decorations, at the Christmas cards lined up on her mantel and the pile of wrapped gifts. She struggled to ignore her heavy heart.

As she tossed the mail on the kitchen counter, Simon's bold handwriting, slanted across a business-size envelope, instantly caught her attention. She grabbed it with both hands. Two or three minutes must have passed before she mustered the courage to tear it open.

With her pulse hammering in her ears, she pulled out a refund check for the total amount of his fee. The check was wrapped in a single sheet of white paper. When she unfolded the sheet, she found it blank.

He'd made the check out to her and in the memo line, he'd written one word: *refund*. She had always assumed he'd keep the money. Perhaps this was the only way he had of relieving his conscience. The only way of saying he had regrets, too. Not knowing just what she'd do with it, Cassie propped the check against the base of a blooming poinsettia—the very one he'd given her. She'd need to think about her response.

She could refuse to cash it out of pure stubbornness. That seemed foolish. When she'd paid Simon, she'd explained that the funds had come from a special savings account, which she'd set up to pay for her wedding. Perhaps he was saying he wanted her to have that wedding.

No, she mused, shaking her head. She couldn't second-guess him, couldn't drive herself insane trying to analyze his motives.

The phone rang and, still absorbed in her thoughts, Cassie picked it up. "Hello," she murmured.

"Hello." The male voice was unfamiliar. "My name is John Fitzsimmons and I was given your number by a...mutual friend."

"What can I do for you, John?" she asked, suspicion springing to life.

"Well...I was hoping we could meet for coffee." He sounded nervous.

"What friend?"

"Ah..."

"Is it Simon?" she asked. It hadn't taken her long to catch on. The matchmaker in him was incapable of letting this go. He'd found the man he believed to be her ideal match. Obviously, Simon was hoping to assuage his guilt by making sure she had the opportunity to meet John—an opportunity she'd already declined.

"Simon suggested it might be better if I implied it was someone else, but I'm not much good at prevarication."

"I'm not, either."

John chuckled. "He said you backed out at the last minute."

"I did," she confirmed.

"I know it's none of my business, but would you mind telling me why?"

Cassie bit her lip and debated how wise it would be to reveal the truth, then decided she owed him that. "I apologize because I realize I let you down, but...unfortunately I fell in love with someone else."

"Oh." She heard a world of disappointment in that one word. He didn't say anything for a moment. "Did you tell Simon this?"

"Yes, I was in his office on Monday." Could that have been just forty-eight hours ago? It seemed far longer; it seemed like a lifetime.

John hesitated again. "Then I don't understand why Simon was so insistent that I call you."

Cassie, however, was completely aware of his motivation. "I'm afraid...well, the man I fell in love with is Simon."

"Oh." There was a wealth of meaning in his short response. "I guess it would be safe to say he doesn't return your feelings?"

Cassie believed he did. "Apparently not," she said softly, hoping the pain she felt wasn't obvious.

"I guess that explains why he urged me to contact you."

She disagreed, but didn't voice her opinion.

"I realize you...like Simon, but seeing that he doesn't feel the same way, it might help if we met. Simon spoke highly of you on several occasions and I thought the two of us might have a lot in common."

"What did he say about me?" she asked.

"Well..." He drew out the word. "He said that you're thoughtful and caring of others."

Despite herself, Cassie smiled. Simon had chosen to forget her negative attitude toward her neighbors and how she'd done everything she could to get out of hosting the pre-Christmas dinner party.

"He said you're wonderful with children."

"He did?" She closed her eyes and remembered the sad little girl who'd come to visit Santa. All that child wanted for Christmas was for her father to come home. Even the hardest heart would've been affected by such a request.

"He also said how generous you are to others."

Cassie wasn't sure that was true.

"And he told me you're one of the most beautiful clients he's ever had the pleasure of working with. He said your beauty is special because it's internal as well as external."

"That was kind of him." Simon would cringe if he heard her say that. He didn't receive compliments gladly.

"Actually, Simon couldn't say enough good things about you. He urged me to ask you out and not to take no for an answer. You will meet me, won't you?"

She probably should but couldn't dredge up any enthusiasm for even a casual meeting. She needed time to deal with her complicated feelings for Simon. Her love was as strong now as when she'd stepped into his office two days earlier, and yet it was useless to believe he'd change his mind.

"I don't know," she said honestly.

"What would it hurt?" John asked. "All I'm suggesting is that the two of us have coffee together."

He had a point, but she hesitated. "It's, uh, nice that you'd still like to meet, especially since you know how I feel about Simon."

"I do. From everything Simon had to say, it sounds as

if we're a perfect match. Or—" and she could hear the smile in his voice "—the most suitable one."

That might've been true a few weeks ago, but it wasn't anymore. She loved Simon.

"I think perhaps we should drop it for now," she said.

To her surprise, John laughed. "Simon told me you'd say that, but he also said I should be persistent."

Cassie straightened and a chill went down her spine. "Did he?"

"Yes. In fact, he said I shouldn't listen to any arguments. He went so far as to say he's introduced dozens of couples over the past few years and in all that time he's never met two people who were a better fit for each other than you and me."

Cassie had to restrain a laugh. Simon was doing his utmost to push her into the arms of another man, and his determination only served to confirm that she'd been right all along.

But telling John this would be touchy. "Why do you suppose he praised me so much?" she asked him.

"Well..."

"I suppose you've noticed that Simon isn't really one for flattery."

"Yeah."

"When I first met him, I wasn't sure what to think."

"Me neither," he said.

"He seemed way too dictatorial."

"I hear a lot of people have the same feeling. The friend who told me about Simon and his matchmaking business said I shouldn't take offense at his gruff manner."

"Did his attitude change?" she asked. "Did he start to react to you in a different way?"

"Not really. Why?"

"He did with me."

"Oh. That's the reason you asked why he had so many wonderful things to say about you, isn't it?"

"Yes."

"So you think he's in love with you, too?"

"I do."

John sighed. "Seems funny, doesn't it, that a matchmaker would have such a hard time admitting he's in love."

Cassie wasn't exactly laughing. "In any other circumstances, you and I would probably have gotten along famously—and maybe even decided to marry."

"Maybe," he concurred. "Who's to know."

"Thank you for calling, John. I want nothing but the very best for you."

"Thanks." He paused and she could hear Elvis Presley's "Blue Christmas" in the background. "I guess this means you're definitely not going out with me."

"That's true."

"Okay."

"Bye." She started to hang up when John stopped her.

"Yes?" she said.

"Cassie, I was wondering if you'd take my phone number—in case you have a change of heart."

"It's in my phone, John. I have it."

"You won't lose it, will you?"

"No, I won't lose it," she promised. "Merry Christmas, now."

Late the following day, Christmas Eve, Cassie was grateful for Mrs. Mullinex's invitation. She hated the idea of spending the evening alone.

Although she wasn't Catholic, she thought she might attend midnight mass at the cathedral after that. The beauty of the service and the music would lift her heart and infuse her with holiday spirit.

The small get-together at Mrs. Mullinex's was congenial, with Harry and Phyllis exchanging fond smiles over their fruitcake and eggnog. Love seemed to be blossoming all around her. First Shawn and Angie, and now her two cantankerous neighbors.

She toasted her newfound friends and after a respectable length of time made her excuses. They all hugged and wished each other a Merry Christmas, and she did the same.

As she left she saw a male figure heading toward the elevator. From behind he resembled Simon. He was about to step through the elevator doors when she called his name.

"Simon?"

He turned abruptly, a frown darkening his face.

"What are you doing here?" she asked.

"Why did you turn John Fitzsimmons down?"

"I think you know," she said calmly.

"You're a stubborn woman."

"You mean you've only noticed that now?" She unlocked her door and entered the apartment.

After a moment's hesitation, Simon followed her inside.

Chapter 17

Simon says: The perfect Christmas is the one I spend with you.

Simon strode into Cassie's apartment but couldn't seem to stop moving, from door to window and back again.

Cassie wished she dared to throw her arms around him and halt his frantic pacing.

"Why wouldn't you agree to at least meet John?" The anger seemed to radiate from him.

"Simon, you know why. I'm in love with you."

His eyes slammed shut and he clenched his jaw. "I don't want your love."

"So you said." That didn't change the way she felt, though.

"What harm would it have done to meet John?"

"None, I suppose," she said with a shrug. "But I felt I would've been doing him a disservice."

It was as though he hadn't heard her. "In other words, despite your assurances that you're willing to move on with your life, you refuse to do so," he challenged.

Cassie sat on her sofa while Simon continued pacing. She tracked his movements with her eyes. "Don't worry. I'll date other men—when I'm ready."

He whirled around and glared at her.

Cassie felt it was her turn to pose a few questions. "Why are you fighting this?" she asked, looking up at him. "And...why are you here at all?"

"I had to talk to you about John." Simon shook his head. "Don't you realize marrying *me* would be a disaster?"

"Really?" It didn't escape her notice that he hadn't denied anything—and that he'd brought up marriage. Evidently the subject had been on his mind, which was encouraging. "Why's that?"

Simon abruptly stood still. "I suspect I'm not telling you anything you don't know. I'm not...comfortable with emotions on a personal level. I prefer to analyze and guide other people's emotional lives. I have a hard time admitting this, but I've always steered clear of the intensity, the giving up of control...." He sounded so unlike the confident, self-assured man she'd come to know, and his vulnerability made him even more appealing.

"I hate this confusion," he muttered. "I'm good at helping my clients sort through their feelings, good at writing about them—but not good at experiencing them. It makes me...miserable."

"I've been pretty miserable myself," Cassie said.

"Then we should both find ways of dealing with these emotions because I'm not changing my mind."

"So you've said."

"I mean it, Cassie."

She wasn't going to argue. "Yes, I know."

He stared at her, eyebrows raised. "Don't be so agreeable. I'm not used to it, and I don't know how to react when you're amenable to everything I say."

She nodded.

"See? That's what I mean." He pointed accusingly at her. "Listen. I know what kind of man makes a good husband—and I'm not it."

Cassie had to smile. "That's something I *don't* agree with. You've shown me truths about myself. Let me do the same for you."

Simon shook his head as if that possibility was beyond him.

Cassie wasn't about to let him assume he was incapable of love when she knew otherwise.

She stood and walked purposefully toward him. He was still pacing, so she caught his hand. Her fingers curled around his and he turned back to stare at her. Not giving him a chance to object, she leaned forward and placed her mouth on his.

Simon slipped one hand around the back of her head and kissed her with a hunger that thrilled her.

"We'll start with teaching you to accept my love," she whispered when he broke off the lengthy kiss.

Again he briefly closed his eyes.

"Love is one thing," he muttered. "But you want children. I don't know about children except in theory. I'm not good with them," he said. "They cry and make messes in their diapers and drool."

"That they do."

"I don't understand why people willingly submit

themselves to the uncertainty and stress of raising children." He splayed his fingers through his hair.

Even as he spoke she heard the longing in his voice. Despite his claims to the contrary he desired a family, just like most people did. Just like *she* did. Unable to resist a moment longer, she slid her arms around his waist and hugged him close. He resisted at first and attempted to break free.

Cassie held tight. Smiling up at him, she stood on the tips of her toes, rested her hands on his shoulders and pressed her mouth to his. It was only a matter of seconds before he became fully involved in the kiss.

When her legs were about to give way, Simon tore his mouth from hers and stepped back, still holding on to her, which was a good thing. Otherwise Cassie would have collapsed in a heap on the floor.

He wagged a warning finger at her. "No more of that."

"Sorry." She felt she should probably apologize but giggled instead. "I couldn't help myself. Oh, Simon, you're right. I do want children—your children. We'll have very special babies."

His expression was wry. "They won't cry and make messes and—"

"Of course they will," she said, nudging him.

"Like I already said, I have no skills in this area."

"But I don't, either. We'll learn together, the way other parents do."

She wasn't sure if she'd convinced him or not because he continued to stare at her.

Then, as if he'd noticed the Christmas decorations for the first time, he frowned and said, "When you came to me, you talked about a perfect Christmas."

She nodded.

"I'm not big on Christmas."

"I think that's kind of a weak argument," she told him. "Seeing how every assignment you gave me had to do with the holidays."

"Only because there's a surfeit of them at this time of year."

"True, but there are plenty of others and you *chose* the Christmas-related tasks."

"You've found some hidden meaning in that?"

"Yes. It's obvious to me that you enjoy the holidays."

When he started to protest, she held up a hand.

"Let me amend that. You enjoy watching other people enjoy Christmas. You understand why it's important to them, the same way you understand—in theory—

why love and marriage and children are important. If you don't like Christmas, it's because you're alone. You don't have anyone to share it with. But, Simon, that's about to change."

"Aren't you making assumptions you have no business making?"

"Is this really so difficult?" she asked.

"Yes," he groaned.

Cassie gently laid her head against his chest and sighed meaningfully.

His sigh echoed hers. "Oh, I give up. You knew I'd fallen in love with you." He drew her toward him and rested his chin on her head.

"I *hoped* so."

"I do love you, Cassie."

"And I love you."

He leaned down and shattered what remained of her composure with a single kiss.

"You seriously want to marry me?" he whispered.

"More than I've wanted anything in my entire life."

"And children. You want children."

She nodded, knowing he wanted them as much as she did. "Two or three, at least."

He closed his eyes.

"You're going to be a wonderful father. And a wonderful husband."

"Our babies are going to inhabit my heart the same way you have. I see it happening already." He gazed down at her with such tenderness it nearly brought tears to her eyes.

"Inhabit your heart," she repeated. "And you've moved into mine."

"I couldn't forget you for even a second," he whispered, holding her close and breathing the words against her hair. "I'm not sure what it is about you that's different from all the other women I've met, the other women who fell in love with me...or thought they did. I just know you were right when you told me I loved you."

His arms tightened around her. "You're right about Christmas, too."

"I figured as much."

"Am I so easy to read?"

"No."

"We're going to have a very good life together," he murmured. "And every Christmas—"

Her phone rang, interrupting him. Cassie was content to let it ring until Simon released her.

Checking call display, she said, "It's my brother."

"You should answer it."

Nodding, she reached for the receiver. "Hello, Shawn."

"Merry Christmas." Shawn's greeting sounded happier than she could remember hearing in a long, long time.

"Merry Christmas," she said in return.

"You seem happy… Any particular reason?"

"Simon's here."

Shawn hooted with laughter. "He couldn't hold out, could he?"

"Thankfully, no. Christmas came early for me."

"Me, too," Shawn said. "Come and join us, both of you."

Half an hour later, the four of them sat in front of a crackling fire in Angie's small rental house in West Seattle. The clock above the mantel chimed midnight.

"It's Christmas," Angie sang out as she leaned against Shawn.

Simon's arm was around Cassie's shoulder. "Christmas," she echoed. Then she spoke softly into his ear. "My *perfect* Christmas, Simon. I have it right here, right now, with you."